MAN DOWN

Hardy hurled himself sideways and felt the wind of passing lead. A slug burned a streak along his ribs. He jerked his guns and shot with both hands as fast as he could pull the trigger. Answering shots streaked lances of light through the gloom. The building rocked to the roar of the reports.

Ducking, weaving, trying to keep out of a direct line with the open door, Hardy fired again and again. He heard a coughing grunt, then the thud of a falling body.

And at the same instant, Cliff Hardy's head seemed to explode in one vast burst of fire and pain. He felt himself falling and clutched at the wall for support. Instinctively his fingers tightened on the triggers of his sagging guns. One boomed a last shot. The other clicked on an empty shell. Hardy was sliding down the wall, clawing vainly at the smooth surface. His guns clattered to the floor and he sank beside them in a motionless heap.

Other *Leisure* books by Bradford Scott:

TEXAS RANGER
TERROR STALKS THE BORDER

PANHANDLE PIONEER

Bradford Scott

LEISURE BOOKS NEW YORK CITY

A LEISURE BOOK®

August 2008

Published by special arrangement with Golden West Literary Agency.

Dorchester Publishing Co., Inc.
200 Madison Avenue
New York, NY 10016

ISBN 10: 0-8439-6106-6
ISBN 13: 978-0-8439-6106-5

The name "Leisure Books" and the stylized "L" with design are trademarks of Dorchester Publishing Co., Inc.

Printed in the United States of America.

10 9 8 7 6 5 4 3 2 1

Visit us on the web at www.dorchesterpub.com.

PANHANDLE PIONEER

ABOUT THE AUTHOR

Bradford Scott was born in Lewisburg, West Virginia. During the Great War, he joined the French Foreign Legion and spent four years in the trenches. In the 1920s he worked as a mining engineer and bridge builder in the western American states and in China before settling in New York.

A barroom discussion in 1934 with Leo Margulies, who was managing editor for Standard Magazines, prompted Scott to try writing fiction. He went on to create two of the most notable series characters in Western pulp magazines. In 1936, when Standard Magazines launched *Texas Rangers*, Scott, under the house name of Jackson Cole, created Jim Hatfield, Texas Ranger, a character whose popularity was so great with readers that this magazine featuring his adventures lasted until 1958.

When others eventually began contributing Jim Hatfield stories, Scott created another Texas Ranger hero, Walt Slade, better known as El Halcón, The Hawk, whose exploits were regularly featured in *Thrilling Western*.

In the 1950s Scott moved quickly into writing book-length adventures about both Jim Hatfield and Walt Slade in long series of original paperback Westerns. At the same time, however, Scott was also doing some of his best work in hardcover

Westerns published by Arcadia House: thoughtful, well-constructed stories, with engaging characters and authentic settings and situations. Among the best of these are *Silver City* (1953), *Longhorn Empire* (1954), *The Trail Builders* (1956), and *Blood on the Río Grande* (1959). In these hardcover Westerns, Scott proved himself highly capable of writing traditional Western stories with characters who have sufficient depth to change in the course of the narrative and with a degree of authenticity and historical accuracy absent from many of his series stories.

CHAPTER I

When Cliff Hardy rode out of Ragtown, later to be Amarillo, the metropolis of the Texas Panhandle, people stared and shook their heads.

Not that there was anything unusual in a cowhand in Levis, high-heeled boots, dimpled, broad-brimmed "J.B." and faded blue shirt, with double cartridge belts encircling his lean waist and Colt Forty-fives sagging the holsters, riding either into or out of Ragtown.

But when said cowhand rode on the seat of a big freighting wagon drawn by six shambling, heavy-headed horses, with a splendid red sorrel bearing full riding rig pacing sedately behind the tail gate of the wagon, *that* was something to stare at.

Hardy didn't know where he was going, and he didn't particularly care. He just felt like riding. In fact, he didn't have any place much to go. He had quit his job of riding for the Bar A Ranch the day before, after punching the range boss in the nose, very much to the detriment of the nose. When Cliff Hardy hit a man, he was *hit*.

Hardy had ridden into Ragtown the previous afternoon with his saddle horse, Rojo, his two guns, and forty dollars in his pocket. Now he had better than two hundred and forty dollars in his pocket and was the owner of a freighting wagon and six horses. He had spent the night at whiskey and poker, and the poker game had proved remunerative. A freighter whose supply of ready cash was exhausted had bet the wagon and team against the two hundred and fifty-odd dollars Hardy had in front of him at the moment. An ace-full doesn't stand up well against four sixes, so the freighter lost his wagon and team. Which didn't bother him particularly— he had more wagons.

The wagon and the team bothered Cliff Hardy somewhat. They were a responsibility, and he was in no mood for responsibilities. He regarded the horses owlishly, raised his slightly bleary eyes and surveyed the prospect ahead.

Mile on mile stretched the sun-drenched prairie, to the ever retreating bowl edge of the horizon. Not a hill, not a tree broke the flat

monotony. No, that wasn't just the right word.
Not with the wind-swept grass rippling in end-
less waves of amethyst-tipped green. This level
rangeland was not monotonous. Its sameness was
the sameness of a many-faceted gem that in itself is changeless but blazes forth with all the
infinite variety of light.

But the eternal sameness made for confusion,
and danger. The roads of the Panhandle, where
it would seem there was no need for roads over a
land flat as a billiard table or gently rolling,
with Nature's perfect "grading," were marked
by furrows plowed in the sod. These indicated
the lines of communication from town to town,
while one extended southward across the State
Line to Roswell, New Mexico. Ranchers blazed
the roads from their ranchhouses in the same
manner, for on the prairies it was easy for a
traveller to become lost.

Cliff Hardy wasn't worried about getting lost;
he had the plainsman's instinct for distance and
direction. Besides, how could you get lost when
you weren't coming from any place and weren't
going anywhere!

Finally, about mid-morning, he saw far ahead
a patch of brush scuffed up like the nap of a
kicked carpet. He eyed it with interest. That
ragged stand of brush must mark the course of

a stream. The brush meant firewood and the stream meant coffee. A swig of that, steaming hot, wouldn't taste at all bad. He slapped the reins and swore pleasantly at the horses. The shambling brutes quickened their pace, doubtless not in deference to the jovial profanity but because they scented water.

But distances are deceptive on the prairie, and an hour elapsed before he could see the stream meandering across the rangeland. As he drew near, he saw that its banks and environs were dotted with white objects, which he identified as the bleached bones of countless buffalo. Coming for water, the great beasts had been mercilessly slaughtered by waiting hunters.

Cliff Hardy had never gone in for buffalo hunting. He had an aversion to killing things that couldn't fight back. Admittedly, an angry bull buffalo was a tough customer and able to make things lively for the Plains Indians with their bows and lances; but against a Fifty-calibre Sharpe's bullet his toughness didn't do him much good. About all the hunter had to fear was getting caught in front of a stampede of the terrified beasts. Otherwise the advantage was all on his side.

When he reached the stream Hardy unhitched the team, got the rig off Rojo and turned the critters loose to graze. He collected dry wood and soon had a fire going and coffee boiling. He drank about half the bucket, scalding hot, and felt considerably better. His stomach had ceased grumbling and was in a receptive mood. He hauled out a slab of bacon, half a dozen eggs, carefully wrapped against breakage, and a skillet. The well crisped bacon provided grease in which to fry the eggs. When they were well blackened on both sides and seemingly in a condition to guarantee acute indigestion to a rhinoceros, he sandwiched them between slices of bacon and ate with appetite. Then, after downing the rest of the coffee, he deftly rolled a cigarette with the slim fingers of his left hand, stretched out on the soft mat of buffalo grass and smoked in comfort.

As he smoked, he pondered present conditions; they were not satisfactory. He had two hundred and fifty dollars in his pocket. The wagon and the team might bring a couple of hundred more. But that wouldn't last long, with whiskey, women and cards plentiful in every town. He was out of a job, and jobs of riding weren't so easy to come by in this section right now. Besides, he had built up a reputation which was not an asset to a man in search of steady employment. Ranch owners looked askance at a hand who, if he wasn't always looking for trouble, was certainly not in the habit of side-stepping any that came his way. Hardy recalled what Colonel Charles Goodnight, owner of the great JA Ranch, had said when he'd let him go the year before:

"Hardy, the trouble with you is you're too quick with your guns and your fists. You're always getting into a row with somebody. Cattle raising is a business, and constant turmoil among the hands isn't good for business. That's why I'm letting you go, not just because you shot Jim Clarendon. I dare say you felt you had ample provocation, but the fact remains you didn't have to slap half of Clarendon's teeth out of his mouth and cause him to pull on you. And if that slug had gone a couple of inches lower, Clarendon would be dead. Hardy, I'm going to give you a bit of advice. Cool down; don't be so ready to go on the prod. Sooner or later, the way you're going, you'll find yourself in serious trouble. Oh, I know you've never shot except in self-defense, but you're getting a reputation for being a quick-draw man and always ready to reach. When a man is known to be just a little bit faster and more accurate than most, people are apt to get to thinking that 'self-defense' is being stretched a mite far. The Rangers or vigilance committees have taken care of quite a few 'self-defense' gunslingers. Better take my advice, Hardy."

Cliff Hardy hadn't taken Colonel Goodnight's advice, but he did remember the famous cattleman's words, and sometimes he thought of them.

Right now, for instance. Only yesterday his quick temper had cost him a job riding for a good outfit. And he was honest enough with himself to admit that he hadn't had to break the range boss' nose. He could have turned and walked away, even though he had been right and the other wrong. Then the whole incident would have been quickly forgotten and he would still have been riding for the Bar A. As it was, his rope was dragging.

Hardy rolled another cigarette and absently regarded the buffalo skeletons littering the prairie for as far as the eye could reach. There were thousands of them, falling apart, sinking into the grass. Well, they'd do some good, anyhow. Under the beat of the wind, rain and sun, they would crumble, rot, disintegrate and enrich the soil. No better fertilizer than bones.

Suddenly Cliff Hardy leaned forward, his eyes glowing. He stared at the litter of bones as if he had never seen such things before. Then he remarked aloud to the red sorrel, who was grazing nearby:

"Horse, I've got an idea!"

Rojo did not appear impressed.

"Yes, I've got an idea, one that I believe will pay off," Hardy repeated. "I wonder why somebody hasn't already thought of it. Maybe somebody has, but not in this section, that's for certain."

He pinched out his cigarette, made sure the fire could do no damage, and proceeded to put the idea into execution. The scandalized Rojo raised his head and regarded his master in mild astonishment. Cliff Hardy was lugging bones across the prairie and dumping them in the wagon.

Hardy worked all afternoon, packing the wagon carefully. He improvised sideboards with thigh bones and huge shoulder vanes and heaped the load high. By sundown he estimated he had the wagon loaded with fully a ton of bones, about all the team could conveniently haul. He made camp by the stream, and with the first light the following morning set out for Ragtown.

When Cliff Hardy drove into Ragtown, the citizenry stared again. Now they had seen all there was to be seen. There was no doubt in any mind but that the tall cowboy with the black hair and gray eyes was plumb loco. They had suspected something of the sort when he had driven out of Ragtown the day before; now they were certain of it.

Hardy paid no attention to the stares. He hitched his team and proceeded to the railroad station. There he sent a telegram to a seed and fertilizer company in Fort Worth. The telegram read:

"Have two thousand pounds of bones ready for shipment. Prime for fertilizer. What am I offered?"

After this he repaired to the nearest saloon for a drink and something to eat, and to await developments.

During a visit to Fort Worth, Hardy had seen a fertilizer mill in operation, grinding beef bones from the slaughterhouse, and had heard the mill superintendent complain that he couldn't get enough bones to meet the demand for fertilizer.

A couple of hours later a reply came from Fort Worth:

"Three cents a pound. We pay freight and will arrange for shipment. Can use all you send."

And that was the beginning of the great bone-gathering industry that kept Ragtown roaring for several years.

CHAPTER II

Cliff Hardy shipped his bones and a day later rolled out of Ragtown to gather another load. He figured he could easily clear fifty dollars a day at the business of gathering bones. Which, compared with forty per month as a cowhand, was something to think about.

Although he didn't really need to drive all the way to the stream—the bones were bleaching on the range all over the Panhandle—there was a great concentration on the banks of the creek, which made the work easier and faster. The day after he left Ragtown he was back again, his wagon heaped high. The contents were loaded into a waiting freight car and Hardy hurried away for more.

It took the citizens of Ragtown only a few weeks to realize that the tall cowhand, the Bone Picker, as they derisively dubbed him, had uncovered a gold mine, and but a little longer to tumble to the fact that he had by no means cornered the market. There were more bones available than one man could collect in a lifetime. Wagons rolled out of Ragtown in every direction.

Hardy had known from the beginning that others would quickly understand the commercial value of the myriad skeletons dotting the prairie. Before the general rush began, he bought two more wagons and hired a driver for each. He was really setting himself up in business. Then he hired a third driver so that he would be free to put into effect a plan he had evolved during the nights spent beside his lonely campfire.

At that time, much Texas rangeland could be bought for about twenty cents an acre. Hardy rode far and wide on the prairie till he discovered a section where there was an enormous quantity of bones covering a wide area. He negotiated with the Land Office for a thousand acres. With the assistance of one of his drivers, he measured off the plot, utilizing the time-honored method of "rope surveying."

Rope surveying is not very accurate, but it was accepted in the early days of the cattle country. Two men ride over the land selected, each holding one end of a sixty-foot rope. Alternately they forge ahead, and each time the rope comes taut, sixty feet of ground have been covered. Of course a horse doesn't halt instantly, and usually each rope length runs to considerably more than sixty feet. However, the measure was seldom if ever questioned.

So Hardy measured off his lines, set his corner monuments and located the plot in relation to accepted landmarks. The data was sent to the Land Office with the purchase price, and Cliff Hardy, less than a month before a penniless cowhand, was the owner of a respectable hunk of rangeland.

Responsibility sometimes changes a man strangely. Cliff Hardy had lived from one day to the next, taking a full measure from each twenty-four hours, giving little heed to the morrow, and none at all to next week, next month or next year. Now all of a sudden he was thinking in terms of the future.

Hardy knew that bone picking couldn't go on forever. Just as the buffalo had disappeared from the prairies, so in time would the bones they had left behind. But the land with its thick mat of succulent buffalo grass would remain. He had increased his wagons to twenty and was making money. And as fast as he made it, he spent it for land and still more land. Before two years had passed he owned more than a hundred thousand acres on either side of the creek that wound through a treasure trove of bones. His last purchase pushed his holdings into the rough and broken country that bordered the Canadian River. Here were ravines that would provide shade in summer and protection against blizzards in winter.

For Cliff Hardy knew that something else was coming into the Panhandle country, and coming to stay. As yet there were few cattle ranches on the vast rolling plains. The country of the Nueces, the Trinity and the Brazos was as yet the great cattleland of Texas; but the lands to the south and the east were becoming, comparatively speaking, "crowded." It was requiring more and more acreage to provide sustenance for a cow. In fact, in some parts it was thought best not to put more than fifty cows on a section of 640 acres.

Here things were different. Hardy estimated the range would support two hundred head to the square mile. Thus his better than a hundred thousand acres would take care of a large herd.

The most prevalent grass in the region was buffalo grass, not much to look at green or cured. Seldom more than six inches tall, it spreads something like moss. Its growing season starts in earliest spring, and it cures on the stock. It is sweeter and more nutritious in the fall and winter than any other time, and it is little affected by the continuous pounding of hoofs and steady grazing. It comes up just the same year after year. There was also blue joint, tall and thick, succulent gramma-grass and needle and wheat. Here was what many other cattle-raising sections lacked—year-round forage.

So, figuring he had sufficient land for the present, Hardy began saving his money. He concentrated on bone picking and held his other plans in abeyance.

The bone picking industry was booming. All over the Panhandle and beyond, the prairie was dotted with men and wagons. Disputes arose over choice spots, and were sometimes settled through gunsmoke. Questionable characters began to appear on the scene; men who were not interested in picking bones, but were looking for "bones" to pick. Honest collectors began packing rifles as part of their equipment.

The citizens of Ragtown and its environs respected Cliff Hardy's markers and refrained from encroaching on his property. It was not so with others. In addition to his wagoneers and their helpers, Hardy hired guards to patrol his lines. Several times poachers were warned away. It was not until some time later that serious trouble developed. And when it did, Hardy was in the middle of it.

Having already had experience with poachers, Hardy was not particularly surprised one afternoon to see three men walking along the banks of the creek, apparently estimating the possible harvest of bones available, for they kept pointing and gesturing, pausing from time to time to study their surroundings. He noted one make a wide gesture that seemed to embrace the rugged country through which the stream flowed to join the Canadian River.

Hardy was riding alone, but that did not deter him from approaching the trio. He had encountered such before, and after a brief discussion had always been able to put his point across. The bone hunters had looked hungrily at the deposits but had invariably departed empty-handed, albeit sometimes reluctantly.

As he drew near Hardy noted that one of the men, whose horses stood patiently nearby with drooping heads and trailing split reins, was short and stocky. Another was a tall, well set-up man with grizzled hair and a square, expressionless face. He had keen eyes and a tight mouth.

The third man caught and held Hardy's attention. He was lean and long, with scrawny hips and drooping shoulders. His arms, very long, hung loosely by his sides. His face was cadaverous, with a long blue chin, narrow eyes set deep in his head and a mouth that was a red, reptilian slit between his sunken cheeks. Hardy noted that he wore two guns slung very low, and that the bottoms of the holsters were tied down, so that the leather sheaths would remain rigidly in place when their owner "reached." Hardy recalled once hearing an old peace officer remark that men with tied-down holsters didn't usually live long.

"That's the mark of a professional gunman who's always looking for trouble," the oldster had said. "Sooner or later they find it; usually sooner."

The stocky man also wore a gun, but the third, the big man with grizzled hair, was apparently unarmed. He was dressed in black relieved only by the snowy white of his ruffled shirt front, and he smoked a cigar. The others wore the conventional overalls and faded blue shirts of the rangeland.

As Hardy approached, the trio turned to face him. He noted that the lanky man moved a couple of steps to one side. Hardy dismounted and walked forward slowly. He paused when he was about ten paces distant.

"Howdy, gents," he said. "Something on your mind?"

The lanky man looked him over before speaking; then he said, in a harsh, rasping voice:

"We aim to do a little bone picking hereabouts."

Hardy shook his head. "Sorry," he replied, "but this is private property. You can't pick here."

The grizzled man and his companion remained silent. The lanky man leaned forward a little, his bony hands swinging just a trifle closer to his sides.

"Feller," he said, "this has always been open range and it's going to stay open range. We don't aim to have any nesters squatting here."

His tone was belligerent, edged by an insolent contempt.

Hardy was a bit taken aback at the unexpected answer. Instantly he realized that for some reason the man was deliberately seeking to force a quarrel. He wondered why. His own quick temper was rising, but he held it in leash for the moment. He could be mistaken, and a moderate approach might prevent trouble.

"I'm not a nester," he said. "My land is bought and paid for. If you'd looked when you rode in you'd have seen my markers, if you aren't plumb blind. If you doubt what I tell you, you can check at the courthouse in Ragtown."

"We're not checking anywhere, and we're not taking any nester's word for anything," the other replied. "We aim to pick bones here and we're going to. And now you get back where you come from or it'll be the worse for you."

Cliff Hardy saw he was in for it. It was either back down or have real trouble. He didn't intend to back down.

"Feller," he said, his voice brittle, "you are on private property, a trespasser. Don't forget: it's paid for. Now you get going, and get going fast. And if you're looking for trouble, I'll give it to you till it runs out of your ears. Get going, I said."

A thin grin of satisfaction seemed to twist the other's mouth. He reached!

He was fast. Cliff Hardy had never seen a faster draw. But *he wasn't quite fast enough!*

Cliff Hardy shot from the hip, again and again, the reports blending in a drumroll of sound.

The lanky man reeled back as if struck by a giant fist. His gun exploded and the bullet plowed into the sod at Hardy's feet. Had the situation been less grim, his expression would have been ludicrous—an expression of horrified disbelief. He tottered, the gun dropping from his nerveless hand, and fell as a tree falls, onto his face to lie twitching, his life draining out through his shattered lungs. Cliff Hardy had killed his first man.

Hardy's left-hand gun menaced the other two, who made no move. The grizzled man did not appear particularly affected by what had happened. He rolled his cigar from one corner of his mouth to the other, blew out smoke, and looked Hardy up and down, slowly and carefully.

His stocky companion was white to the lips, his open mouth forming a silently shrieking O.

"You killed him!" he gasped.

"Reckon I did," Hardy returned, glancing at the body which no longer moved. "All right, load him on his horse and pack him in to the sheriff. You can tell your story to *him*. Tell him I'll tell mine when he rides out after me; I'll be right here. Get going!"

The stocky man shivered and shrank from the corpse, but the other strode to the body, picked it up, apparently without effort, and draped it across the saddle of one of the horses. He secured it in place with a tie rope, and broke the silence for the first time, rumbling something to his companion that Hardy did not catch. Then he mounted and rode off, leading the horse with its grisly burden, the stocky man riding beside him. Neither looked back.

Gazing at the jolting, flopping body, Cliff Hardy suddenly experienced a sickish feeling in the pit of his stomach. Abruptly he recalled something Colonel Goodnight said to him a couple of years before:

"Keep on going the way you're headed and you'll find out what others have found out before you: that a dead man doesn't make a soft pillow at night."

At the time, Hardy had thought the old cattle king's words a bit bombastic; now he wasn't so sure.

CHAPTER III

To Hardy's surprise, Sheriff Frank Nance did not show up at his holdings. After two days had passed, curiosity sent him riding to Ragtown.

When he entered the sheriff's office, Nance, a gray and weather-beaten old-timer and an associate of G. W. "Iron-hand" Arrington, the famous Texas Ranger Captain, was working at his desk. He nodded, waved his visitor to a chair and went on with the letter he was writing. Finally he folded the sheets and thrust them into an envelope.

"Well, what's on *your* mind?" he asked.

Hardy told him. The sheriff listened, tugging his mustache, until he had finished.

"Nobody showed up here with any bodies," he said. "Describe the man you shot again."

Hardy did so. The sheriff looked thoughtful.

"Judging from your description, I'd say it was Gulden Blain, as poisonous a reptile as ever crawled out of a hole in the spring," he said. "I'm not surprised that nobody brought him here. He was a professional killer and said to have the fastest gun hand in this end of Texas; apparently he didn't. Now go over everything again and tell me just what was said, and describe the big fellow again, too, real careful."

Hardy obeyed. The sheriff looked even more thoughtful, especially as Hardy detailed the big grizzled man.

"And that," said the sheriff, "was Basset Shaw, sometimes called 'Silent' Shaw. He owns a saloon and gambling hall over in Tascosa. Came there from Dodge City, where he owns more property and built up considerable of a reputation as a mighty cold proposition."

"He was sure silent out there on the prairie," Hardy conceded. "Didn't open his mouth once, until he got ready to ride away. Then he said about two words to the other jigger; I didn't catch what he said."

"Reckon you couldn't," agreed the sheriff. "Nobody hears what Silent Shaw says except whoever he's talking to. But the jigger he's talking to hears, and listens."

"What I can't understand is why that hellion

was so anxious to kill me," Hardy remarked.

"Hardy," said the sheriff, "I'm of a notion he had no intention of killing you; not just then, anyhow."

"No?" Hardy was plainly incredulous.

"No," answered the sheriff. "Gulden Blain was so fast with a gun that I'm of the opinion he figured he could get the drop on you easy, and then you'd have to listen when he talked turkey. 'Pears he made a little mistake, and paid for it in the way his kind usually pays when they make mistakes."

Sheriff Nance was silent for some minutes, while Hardy waited expectantly.

"There's something mighty funny about this business," the sheriff said at length. "Yes, mighty funny. Nobody can tell me that Basset Shaw intends to go in for bone picking. That ain't his style at all. Bone picking pays off, but to a man of Shaw's calibre it's just chicken feed. When Shaw goes after something, it's something big. Now I wonder what that tight-latigoed rapscallion has in mind. Let me think a bit."

There followed another period of silence, while Hardy smoked and the sheriff sat deep in thought. Abruptly he asked a question.

"As I understand it, your holdings over there are long and narrow, on either side of the creek and on into the rough country this side of the Canadian River?"

"That's right," Hardy admitted.

"So as the situation stands, you've fenced in, as it were, about the only worthwhile water for a good many miles."

"Guess that's right, too, although I never thought of it in just that light," Hardy conceded.

"And no matter how good the grass is, you can't raise cows without water."

"I considered that when I acquired the land," Hardy said. "The way my holdings run, every acre of it is easily accessible to water."

"Which brings us to the point," said the sheriff. He was silent again, tugging his mustache.

Like many of the stern peace officers of his day, Sheriff Frank Nance was a religious man. He attended church whenever he happened to be where there was a church, and he read his Bible assiduously. Now he drew a battered volume from a drawer and began thumbing the pages.

"Hmmm! here it is," he said, and read in a sonorous voice:

"And Isaac's servants digged in the valley, and found there a well of springing water.

"And the herdmen of Gerar did strive with Isaac's herdmen, saying, The water is ours. . . .

"And they digged another well, and strove for that also. . . .

"And he removed from thence, and digged another well; and for that they strove not. . . ."

"And that," said Sheriff Nance, closing the Book, "is an account of the first range war of which we have any record. When Isaac with his many flocks and herds went into the Valley of Gerar to dwell, he immediately got into a row with the other cattlemen there and had no peace till he trailed his twine away from there. And what was the row over? Over what usually starts trouble in a dry country—water!"

"Meaning?" Hardy asked.

"Meaning," said the sheriff, "that you've got control of the water upon which a considerable section of fine grazing land is dependent. As I said, you've fenced it in, and the land on either side of your holdings is worthless for cattle raising without it."

"But," protested Hardy, "there's plenty of water. I wouldn't shut out my neighbors, if I happened to get some; they could run ditches and get all they need."

"Uh-huh, and now we come right down to the nubbin of the ear," said the sheriff. "You could charge, and charge plenty, for every drop of water you turned from the creek that is part of your holdings."

"But I wouldn't!" Hardy exploded.

"Nope, I don't suppose you would," conceded the sheriff. "But if somebody else controlled that creek as you do, *they* might charge. And there's another angle to consider. The land on either side of your holdings can be mighty cheap right now. And I'm predicting that soon that land will bring a darned sight better price. Buying that land right now and being able to promise water for it would be a mighty sound investment. Most folks, even some who should, don't appreciate what's going to happen in this Panhandle plains country in the next few years. Some with vision do, and I predict some of those few are going to get set to make a prime killing in the near future."

The sheriff paused to refill and light his pipe and then resumed:

"I reckon you've heard—everybody has—that a while back an outfit known as the Capitol Syndicate Company agreed to build a new state-house at Austin in return for a big strip of land two hundred miles long running down the New

Mexico Border through ten Panhandle counties. When they finish with it, it'll be the biggest cattle ranch in the world. They've already begun fencing that land and running in cows from Tom Green County. They're focusing attention on the Panhandle, and mighty soon cows are going to pour in from every part of the state. I've been saying that for a long time. Folks laughed at me. Some are still laughing, but not so loud. They're beginning to admit that maybe the cattle business in the Panhandle is going to boom. It is."

The sheriff paused, leaned forward and tapped his desk with a finger. "And now we come to how all this bears on you," he said impressively. "When you acquired your holding, I reckon without any intention of doing so, you got the jump on somebody. The value of range is measured by the accessible water. Anyone controlling the water supply practically controls all the contiguous country."

"I only figured on getting a spread of my own," Hardy said.

"Well, you've got it— the land, anyhow," agreed the sheriff. "But you succeeded in getting a lot more. All of a sudden you find yourself sitting in the driver's seat, but I predict you'll find it an awful hot seat before all's finished."

Hardy's lips tightened a little. "I own that

land and I aim to hold onto it," he said quietly.

"And there you're certainly within your legal rights," the sheriff answered. "But you may have trouble holding onto it, and holding onto your life, too."

"I aim to hold onto both," Hardy said, and went back to his bone picking.

CHAPTER IV

Bone picking was becoming a bit more complicated. Bones were rapidly getting scarcer, and with good reason. The Staked Plains and the prairie land to the north, east and west were dotted with the wagons of the bone pickers. Bone picking had become big business. One bone-buying firm estimated that they bought over a seven year period bones that accounted for more than six million buffalo skeletons, and it was but one of many. An account in a Topeka newspaper stated that the bones shipped during the period would have filled a string of forty-foot freight cars more than eight thousand miles long, twice the distance from New York to San Francisco, with enough cars left over to make a "short" train extending from New York to Chicago.

Cliff Hardy, who kept abreast of the times,

rightly read the signs of a tremendous expansion
in the bone picking business, coupled with a
growing scarcity of buffalo skeletons. Witness
advertisements appearing in the newspapers
such as:

1000 TONS OF BONES WANTED
Bickett and Foote, Dealers,

which appeared in the *Dickinson (Dakota)
Press*.

With bones streaming in from every direction,
there was no need for dealers to advertise. Now
they were doing it. A competitive market was
developing.

Yes, bones were not so plentiful and easy to
come by as they once had been. Hardy's wagons
ranged far and wide to get their loads. He had
long abandoned the conventional freight wagons
for specialized vehicles equipped with high,
slatted bone racks which could accommodate a
much greater cargo than a bedded wagon.

And while Hardy owned his land, he still did
not have enough money to stock it properly with
cattle. Also, he desired to buy one more strip
of land, having an uncomfortable premonition
that the time might come when he would badly
need this particular strip. And some farsighted
individual might get ahead of him and place his

holdings in an untenable position.

Uneasy over such a possibility, Hardy negotiated for the strip in question. The price of land was steadily rising and at the moment he didn't have the money to pay for it; but he decided to gamble on the chance that he would be able to negotiate sufficient funds in time.

And then, less than a month after his visit to Sheriff Frank Nance, Hardy made his great find.

Hardy had never explored his northern holdings; he had run his lines to the Canadian River, his northern boundary, and let it go at that. One day, however, he decided to investigate the broken ground to the north. Taking one of his guards as a companion, he rode to the Canadian.

It was a beautiful stream, hardly more than twenty feet wide at this point, with practically no sandbars, the water deep and clear. Its banks were fringed with many bushes and chaparral growth. There was a profusion of wild chokeberries, big plums, wild gooseberries and grapes. There were many cottonwood mottes scattered along the banks. Hardy saw several beaver dams and heard the loud slap of flat tails on the water as the startled little animals warned others that strangers were in their midst.

The terrain south of the Canadian was greatly

cut up by arroyos and canyons leading to the river, some of them heavily grown with chaparral, the floors of others carpeted with heavy buffalo grass.

"Fine places for winter hole-ups against the blizzards," observed Tom Cameron, the guard.

"I thought of that when I bid for this section," Hardy admitted.

Circling to the east, they finally entered a broad and grass-grown ravine that bore north through fairly respectable hills. Cameron scanned the ground with interest.

"A lot of buffalo went through here every now and then," he remarked.

"Headed for the river and water," Hardy guessed.

Cameron, a former cowhand and experienced tracker, continued to scan the ground, his interest growing.

"Funny," he observed. "From the looks of it, I'd say those critters went through here mighty fast. Wonder why? Doesn't look like they'd have been that thirsty; but they sure must have been sifting sand."

"Maybe something scared them," Hardy replied.

"Could be," Cameron conceded. "Me, I'd say there was a regular stampede through here, not once but quite a few times. And it don't look to me like this is a water trail. Those are always worn down deep in the ground, like a big broad ditch. All the marks here are surface cuts."

"Well, we'll keep on riding toward the river and maybe we'll learn something," Hardy said.

A little later they did learn something, and it was a momentous discovery.

The floor of the ravine sloped gently upward. After riding a mile or so they could see, directly ahead, what looked like a clean line of earth and stone running straight across the blue of the slanting northern sky.

"Darned if it don't 'pear to be a jumping-off place up there," said Cameron.

"Be a steep sag down to the river the other side of the ridge, the chances are," Hardy replied.

They quickened their horses' gait, and within a few minutes they reached the end of the ravine. It ended in a sheer wall of rock with a drop of fifty or sixty feet to the floor of a second ravine, narrower and stonier. And scattered over the rocky floor were innumerable white objects. Cameron peered down at those closest to the base of the cliff. He swore an explosive oath.

"Well, I'll be! Boss, do you see what I see?"

"Yes, I think I do," Hardy replied. "Buffalo skeletons!"

"You're right," said Cameron. "I understand

those tracks now. Herd after herd has been stampeded up this gulley and over the cliff."

Hardy nodded. It was a favorite trick of the buffalo-hunting Indians. They would get a herd on the move, ride alongside it, directing the leaders in a certain direction. Soon the whole great herd would be racing frantically to escape. When the leaders reached the lip of a cliff they would plunge over. The remainder of the herd, blindly following the leaders, would also go down to destruction. And the Indians would have all the hides and meat they wanted without shooting an arrow. The white hunters used the same method, and with greater efficiency. Cameron was right. Here vast numbers of the stupid beasts had been stampeded over the cliff to their death on the rocks below.

Cameron ran his eye along the length of the canyon. He gave a loud whistle.

"Boss," he exclaimed excitedly, "there must be a million tons of bones down there!"

"That's a bit hefty," Hardy chuckled, "but there are a good many thousand tons, all right."

Hardy knew he wasn't exaggerating. There had been such finds before. A buyer by the name of McCreight had found a pile at the west end of Devil's Lake, Dakota, that contained nearly three thousand tons, on the southern shore another of nearly two thousand tons, and still another at Mouse River that ran considerably better than three thousand tons.

"And they're all on your land," said Cameron. "Boss, it looks like you won't have to worry about money any more for a while."

"Reckon you won't either," Hardy replied. "We made this find together and of course you'll get a percentage cut."

Cameron gulped and goggled. "Gee—gosh—Boss, that's mighty white of you!" he stuttered.

Hardy grinned a little.

"I'm going to use mine to stock my ranch," he said. "I figure to keep you on with me as range boss, if you care to stay. And, Tom, I'm going to give you a bit of good advice. Don't throw all of yours away on cards and whiskey and women; buy cows with it, and you'll have a stake in the spread and be on the way to something better than range riding at forty per."

Cameron's eyes glowed. "By God, I'll do it!" he exclaimed. "And thanks, Boss, thanks a million!"

"Okay," Hardy said, "and now let's see if we can locate a way into that gulch down there. I've a notion the mouth of it should be over to the west a couple of miles, from the looks of things that way."

After considerable riding around through the gulches and arroyos, they did find an easy way into the canyon. Hardy surveyed it with satisfaction.

"We'll round up all the wagons and run them up here right away," he decided. "It'll be easy loading."

Two days later the great wains were in the canyon, taking on their cargo of bones.

Hardy wasted no time securing title to a strip of land south of his present holdings, after negotiating a bank loan, and felt considerably better. When Sheriff Nance had mentioned that he, Hardy, had "fenced in" the only available water over a wide section, an unpleasant possibility had occurred to him. Suppose someone secured title to the land east and west and south of his holdings and strung wire? All of a sudden *he* would find himself fenced in, with no way of getting his cattle to market. Such things had been done by big owners to freeze out nesters, as they called the small owners who squatted on the open range with a few head of stock.

But now the trail from Ragtown to Forth Worth ran across his southern holding and you couldn't fence an open trail in Texas. He would have an easy route for his drives to the loading pens at Ragtown.

Hardy was, in fact, in a very complacent frame of mind when he rode to the canyon to oversee the loading operations going on there. Nothing more had been heard from Basset Shaw of Tascosa, and no mention had been made of the killing of Gulden Blain. Hardy hadn't talked about it, and neither had Sheriff Nance.

"Guess they got a bellyful out there on the range," Hardy remarked to Nance when he dropped in to see the sheriff one day.

"Don't you think it," grunted Nance. "That isn't Silent Shaw's way. He won't forget. My advice to you is to keep your eyes open. When Basset Shaw goes after something he doesn't stop. He's got some sort of a notion concerning your holdings, and sooner or later he'll move to put that notion into effect. Keep your eyes open, Hardy, or you'll be sorry."

Hardy was inclined to discount the sheriff's warning. After all, he was only twenty-five and hadn't had the old peace officer's experience with questionable characters. He certainly wasn't thinking about Nance's words when he and Tom Cameron rode into the canyon a little before sunset and watched the last big slatted bone rack pull out with its load.

They dismounted, dropped the split reins to the ground and removed the bits so the horses could graze on the rich grass growing between the skeletons. Cameron surveyed the great heaps of bones with satisfaction.

"Ain't hardly made a dent in 'em," he remarked. "Will take weeks for the boys to clean 'em up."

Hardy nodded. He fished out the makings, deftly manipulating tobacco and paper with his left hand. A vagrant puff of wind whipped the tiny paper from between his fingers. He dived forward to retrieve it before it fluttered to the ground. As he did so he heard a queer, choking grunt beside him an instant before the hard, metallic clang of a rifle shot slammed back and forth between the rock walls. Tom Cameron fell forward on his face.

CHAPTER V

For an instant Hardy was paralyzed by the suddenness of it all, but only for an instant. He leaped forward, weaving and ducking, to where his horse stood with pricked ears, staring at the south wall of the canyon.

The rifle cracked again and the slug fanned Hardy's face with its lethal breath. Then he was gripping the stock of the heavy Winchester snugged in the saddle boot on his horse's left side. He slid the long gun free and dived headlong behind a heap of bones. A third bullet knocked chips from a big shoulder vane and ricocheted off into space. Above a clump of brush fringing the canyon wall was a faint bluish mist.

Hardy slung the Winchester underhand. He pulled trigger. Smoke spurted from the rifle muzzle, and the sullen boom sent the echoes to flying again.

An answering shot clattered against the bones. Hardy now saw just where the smoke puffed up. He shifted the rifle muzzle a bit, fired again, and again and again, the ejection lever a blur of movement. Had a cartridge jammed, the stout steel would have shattered like match wood.

At the fifth shot, the clump of brush was violently agitated. Something pitched from it, tumbled over the lip of the cliff and hit the canyon floor with a sodden thud. Hardy jutted his rifle barrel forward to cover the body sprawled on the grass; but the drygulcher did not move. He had evidently been hit dead center. Even if he hadn't, the fall would doubtless have killed him. Hardy concentrated his attention on the brush clump; the hellion might have a companion.

However, nothing moved and the silence remained unbroken. A blue jay came whisking along, the golden light flashing and glinting on its plumage, and settled into the bush: proof positive that nobody was holed up there. Hardy got to his feet and with quick light steps approached the body at the base of the cliffs; he had to make sure of the fellow before turning his attention to Cameron, who still lay motionless where he had fallen.

At close range, a single glance was enough to

tell Hardy that he'd killed his second man; the drygulcher had a blue hole squarely between his glazing eyes. Hardy turned and ran to where Cameron lay. As he drew near, the guard began groaning and rolling his head from side to side. Hardy saw that his face was dyed scarlet by blood. But as he knelt beside the wounded man, to his intense relief he saw that the blood came from a shallow furrow on the left side of Cameron's head, just below the hairline.

"Creased! Just creased!" Hardy muttered thankfully. "Ought to be coming out of it in a minute."

Nearby, a little stream trickled from under the cliff wall. Hardy hurried to it and came back with his hat full of water with which he bathed Cameron's head and washed the caking blood from his face. A moment later the wounded man groaned, opened his eyes and cursed as pain stabbed through them. With Hardy's aid he managed to sit up, holding his throbbing head in his hands.

"What the devil happened?" he mumbled. "What hit me?"

"Fellow up in the bushes there threw a slug at us," Hardy replied. "Reckon if I hadn't stooped down after my cigarette paper at just the right second, I'd have gotten it. Guess it passed right through where my head was a second before, and nicked you."

Cameron swore some more. "Did the side-winder get away?" he asked.

"Nope," Hardy replied. "What's left of him is over there by the cliff. Want to take a look at him? I'll help you. How do you feel?"

"Oh, I'm all right," Cameron returned. "My head hurts and I'm a bit sick at my stomach, but that'll pass. I know; I've been hit a lick before. Lend me a hand."

With Hardy's assistance he got to his feet, rocking a little, and swearing. He shook his head to free his brain of cobwebs and straightened up.

"Okay, let's go," he said. "I want to see that hombre."

"Ornery-looking specimen," he commented a moment later. "A Comanche breed, I'd say. Nope, I don't recollect ever seeing him before. The sort you can hire to do anything for a few dollars. Boss, what the devil's this all about?"

Hardy hesitated, then acquainted Cameron with the incident of a couple of months before, when he had had the run-in with Gulden Blain and Basset Shaw.

"Well, I'll be!" Cameron exploded. "And you kept it to yourself all this time!"

"Wasn't anything to talk about," Hardy replied. "I told the sheriff, and seeing as Shaw didn't do any talking about what happened, why should I?"

"If you'd told me about it sooner, I'd have kept a closer watch over you," Cameron said grimly. "I knew Gulden Blain, and I've heard considerable about Silent Shaw. He's bad medicine. Shaw's back of what happened today, you can bet your last dollar on that."

"Don't you think it might have been one of Gulden's Blain's friends?" Hardy hazarded.

"Gulden Blain's friends, nothing!" snorted Cameron. "That sidewinder never had a friend in his life. Reckon there isn't anybody living who would have lifted a finger to keep him from being downed. No, sir, Basset Shaw's back of this. But why?"

Hardy hesitated again, and then decided to outline for Cameron Sheriff Nance's theory about the "fenced in" water. Cameron was considerably older than himself and had worked for various spreads all over Texas. His experience and his knowledge of the Panhandle and its denizens might prove of value.

Cameron was silent till Hardy finished.

"Nance may have something there," he said then, gingerly exploring his wounded head with his fingertips. "If Basset Shaw has some scheme afoot, he won't stop at anything to get what he wants. Suppose Shaw has bought up or is buying up the land on either side of your holdings. If he had the water you control, he could charge about anything he wanted to for it—all the traffic would bear. See? Just as simple as that. And I reckon he figures the only way to get the water is to get rid of you. What happened today makes it look sort of that way, don't you think?"

"Could be," Hardy admitted. He stared down at the dead man. Strange, today he had not experienced the sickish feeling in the pit of his stomach and the terrible tightening of his nerves that had followed the killing of Gulden Blaine. What had happened today had left him practically unmoved. He didn't like it. Cliff Hardy had no desire to become a killer who could blast out another human's life with indifference. That was one of the things Colonel Goodnight had warned him against. Of course today's killing was justified; he had merely acted to save his own life. But just the same he felt that his emotions should have been more strongly aroused. As it was, the incident had left him cold.

"Don't you think we'd better ride to town and tell the sheriff about this?" Cameron suggested.

"Yes, I reckon we should," Hardy agreed absently, "and have the doctor look at your head."

"Just a scratch," Cameron deprecated the wound. "Didn't much more than cut the skin; but just a graze of a Forty-five slug hits you a hefty wallop. I know; I've been there before. But it don't leave no bad after-effects."

"Just the same, we'll have it looked after," Hardy decided. "Well, if you feel up to it, we'll ride. Guess we'd better leave this horned toad right where he is; the sheriff will want to look him over. Hope the coyotes don't get him before we get back."

"If they do, they'll be poisoned," Cameron growled. "Okay, let's go."

Hardy was gazing at the cliff wall. "Just a minute, Tom," he said. "I believe I can climb up those rocks over to the left."

"Why?" asked Cameron.

"Because that fellow must have had a horse," Hardy explained. "I don't want to leave the poor critter up there with a hull cinched to its back and a bit in its mouth. I'll go up and get the rig off him. Besides, the brand might tell us something."

"Not likely," Cameron answered. "Pretty apt to be a Mexican skillet-of-snakes burn and mean nothing. Careful, now, or you're liable to bust your neck."

Hardy unlooped his sixty-foot rope and hung it around his shoulder. Then he tackled the cliff at a point where there had been a rock fall. Without too great difficulty he reached the summit, and after browsing around a bit he found the horse, tethered to a stout branch. It was a good-looking cayuse with a Pitchfork brand. The Pitchfork, Hardy recalled, was a west New Mexico spread.

That didn't mean much. Saddle horses were sold, or traded, or stolen, and ofttimes showed up a long way from where they were foaled. He removed the rig and turned the animal loose, knowing it would fend for itself till somebody could be sent to bring it in.

Searching in the bushes near the cliff lip, he unearthed the rifle the drygulcher had used, an almost new Winchester. Bundling gun and rig together, he lowered them to the canyon floor by means of the rope and climbed down to rejoin Cameron.

"There's a good hull to pay for your skinned head," he said. "A Brazos tree and nicely stamped leather. And this saddle gun is worth hanging onto. Looks like we came out ahead in the deal. Okay, let's be riding."

When they reached Ragtown it was too late to see the sheriff, and Cameron said he'd be hanged if he was going to wake up the doctor for a pin prick. He put some whiskey on the cut, swore at the sting and let it go at that. Then they had something to eat, a couple of drinks and went to bed.

Early morning found them at the sheriff's office, Cameron apparently none the worse for his mishap. The sheriff listened without comment to what they had to tell him.

"All right," he said, "I'll ride out there with you." He made no mention of the killing during the course of the ride.

Arriving at the canyon, they found the wagoneers, who had discovered the body, conjecturing on what had happened. Hardy satisfied their curiosity with a brief account and left them swearing and casting nervous glances at the cliff tops. In a few minutes, however, they forgot all about it and went back to picking bones.

Sheriff Nance examined the dead man, turned out his pockets and found nothing of significance save a rather large amount of money in gold and silver.

"The price of your scalp," he remarked, jerking his head at Hardy. He tugged his mustache and looked thoughtful.

"Got a feeling I've seen the hellion hanging around the Tascosa saloons," he said. "Comanche breed, from the looks of him; more white blood than red. Load him onto a bone wagon and haul him to town. Should send him right on to the mill to be ground up for fertilizer, but I reckon the coroner will want to hold an inquest and then bury him." He turned to Hardy.

"See what I meant?" he observed.

"Yes, guess I do," Hardy admitted. "It was a nice try."

"And it won't be the last one," the sheriff predicted grimly. "Cliff, you're a marked man."

Hardy shrugged his broad shoulders. "I got a break this time, and maybe I'll get one the next," he replied.

"Maybe." The sheriff did not look convinced.

CHAPTER VI

The attempted drygulching had little effect on Hardy's turbulent bone pickers. Death, sharp and swift, was too common an occurrence on the rangeland for a killing now and then to make much of an impression. The bone pickers and the guards kept their rifles handy, and in the saloons of Ragtown served notice on all and sundry to come ahead and do their darnedest.

Hardy himself became more watchful and Tom Cameron stuck closer to him than a leech. Neither took any more chances than they had to, and they constantly scanned the terrain wherever they happened to be, missing no movement of birds on the wing or little animals in the brush.

"I don't think they'll try it just that way again," Cameron said, "but we'll keep our eyes open for anything that doesn't look just right. That goes for when we're in town, too. Keep your eyes skinned, pardner."

Meanwhile a land developer, Henry B. Sanborn, had laid out a town site around a natural body of water called Amarillo or Wild Horse Lake. There developed a contest for the county seat of Potter County, and when the votes were counted, Amarillo became the county seat. It was said that Sanborn offered the cowboys of the big LX Ranch a town lot each if they would vote for his town; he won an easy victory. The community, which included the first site of Ragtown, was named Amarillo. There was considerable argument as to just what the town owed its name to. Some contended that it was because of its nearness to Amarillo (yellow) Creek, the banks of which were yellow. Others insisted vigorously that the name came from the yellow flowers that blanketed the prairie in spring. Anyhow, the name so pleased promoter Sanborn, who ran a hotel and several business houses, that he had all his buildings painted a bright yellow.

Bone picking had brought great prosperity to Ragtown, now Amarillo, which the arrival of more and more cattle in the section augmented. Lines of cow ponies stood tied to the hitching racks of the main street, and their riders crowded the hotels, bars, gambling houses and restaurants, and rubbed shoulders with the legion of bone pickers, most of whom had themselves been cowhands at one time or another and would be again.

There was no town government and the affairs and laws of the community were administered by Sheriff Nance and his fellow county officials.

Already, Sanborn and J. F. Glidden, who had invented barbed wire back in 1874, had fenced their ranching properties not far from Amarillo with it. And barbed wire "drift" fences were being built to prevent stock from straying south in winter. One such fence was to extend clear across the Panhandle strip.

All of this interested Cliff Hardy. And Hardy had a few novel notions of his own which he planned to put into effect soon.

With the bones along the creek banks and their environs pretty well cleaned out, Hardy did not really require guards to patrol his property; but just the same he kept them on. He had a feeling he might need them. Each day, with Hardy accompanying them, the guards rode in the vicinity of the canyon of bones, keeping watch on the cliff tops and the west mouth of the gorge, which was the only way by which it could be entered, the country at the east end being so scored and cut by gulleys and washes as to make it unapproachable.

The routine of the wagons was to leave Rag-town, or Amarillo, as it was now called, late in the morning and proceed to the canyon. The afternoon was devoted to loading the great racks to capacity. Then the train of nearly thirty vehicles on the average would return to Amarillo, taking advantage of the cool of the evening and early night. The following morning the bones would be loaded into the waiting cars, and the drivers and their assistants would have the rest of the day and that night to do as they pleased. Hardy found that the system worked well and to the satisfaction of all.

Hardy and the guards did not ride from Amarillo with the train, but from the bunkhouse he had built on his holdings close to where he made his initial bone discovery. The guards, ten dependable former cowhands with Tom Cameron in charge, did not discuss their patrol methods with the wagoneers or anybody else.

"This way, if anybody does take a notion to waylay the train, we might be able to get the jump on them," Hardy explained. "The train is my most vulnerable point. Destroy my wagons and it would be considerable of a setback for me. Wagons aren't easy to come by in a hurry right now, and I need the money that's coming in."

"And some hombre, say one that doesn't talk much, might figure that out," growled Tom Cameron. "Boss, you got the right notion."

One evening they were sitting their horses behind a screen of brush near the canyon mouth, watching the long train roll across the prairie westward by slightly south. From the elevation they could see for many miles across the level land.

"Say!" Cameron suddenly exclaimed. "Isn't that horses coming way up there to the northwest?"

"Looks like it," replied Hardy, who had already spotted the bouncing dots advancing on a long slant from the northwest.

The sun had already set, but the evening was very clear, and in the dying light they watched the dots take form and shape.

"A dozen—fifteen of them," muttered Cameron. "Wonder who the devil they could be?"

"Hard to tell," returned Hardy. "Looks like they're headed for that straggle of brush way to the west of here."

In silence they watched the mounted troop ride swiftly through the dying light. It reached the line of chaparral and disappeared from sight. The watchers eyed the far edge of the growth expectantly.

"Why don't they show?" wondered Cameron. "They've had plenty of time to make it through that thicket."

"Tom," Hardy said grimly, "I've a notion

they're not going to show; I believe they're holed up in that brush."

"Huh!" exclaimed Cameron. "And the train will pass right by there!"

"Guess that's the general notion," Hardy agreed.

Cameron swore explosively. "Waiting for the train, eh? Reckon we'd better ride out and tell the boys to hold up."

"I believe I've got a better idea," Hardy replied. "I believe we can ride along in the shadow of the slope, then cut across the range and make it to that thicket without being spotted, especially if the hellions *are* waiting for the train. They'll be all eyes to the front. Then if they are waiting there to make trouble, we can take 'em in the rear and give them a little surprise they won't like."

"It's a long ride," Cameron said dubiously. "Maybe we can't make it in time, if they are up to something."

"I believe we can," Hardy decided. "Anyhow, we'll risk it. Let's go!"

They descended the slope and rode swiftly along its base until they were well to the west of the belt of growth. Then they diagonalled across the prairie, pushing their horses hard. Full dark had descended, and only the wan light of the stars cast a ghostly sheen over the rangeland.

Hardy estimated the distance as the long straggle of growth drew near. They could not see the wagon train, or anything else, for that matter, save the black bristle of the chaparral ahead.

"Close enough," Hardy said in low tones. "We'll leave the horses here; don't want them to hear us coming or we'll be the ones to get the surprise. Let's go; we've got no time to waste."

They dismounted and stole forward on foot, crouching low, peering and listening. They reached the thicket without anything happening and began worming their way through the growth, taking care not to make the slightest sound.

"I heard a bit iron jingle," Hardy whispered to Cameron. "They're in there, all right."

"And I hear the wagons coming," Cameron whispered back. "Easy; we must be getting close."

The popping of harness and the creak of wheels were becoming louder. And still they could see nothing of the ambushers, if they really were holed up at the far edge of the growth. And then there was a sudden burst of flame directly ahead; somebody had ignited a bundle of oil-soaked waste or rags. They heard the startled exclamations of the teamsters as a voice shouted harshly:

"Hands up, you buzzards! Elevate, I say!

Okay, come down off those seats, on this side. Keep your hands up and be careful how you move."

By the glare of the burning waste, Hardy could see shadowy figures at the edge of the growth, guns menacing the huddled teamsters.

"Let 'em have it!" he roared.

He began shooting with both hands. The others fired as fast as they could pull trigger.

A pandemonium of yells and curses arose, then an answering blast of gunfire. A guard yelped with pain as a slug drilled his arm. Another swore viciously, reeling back with blood pouring from his bullet-gashed cheek. The light was dying down and the guns spurted red flashes through the gloom. Crouching low, the guards continued to shoot as a prodigious crashing sounded in the growth.

"They've got their horses!" Cameron shouted. "After 'em!"

The drygulchers had indeed mounted and were fleeing in every direction, speeded on their way by whining lead. Outside the brush, the bewildered teamsters were adding their bellows to the uproar.

"Out of this. Get our bronks!" Hardy shouted. "We'll ride 'em down."

He led the rush out of the growth. As they

burst through the last fringe they saw a clump of horsemen speeding across the prairie. They ran to where they had left their horses and flung themselves into saddles. A moment later and they were in hot pursuit of the fleeing band.

But very quickly they realized that the fugitives had all the best of it. Their horses were comparatively fresh, while those of Hardy and his companions had just finished a hard gallop. Before a mile was covered they were blowing, and falling behind fast.

"No use." Hardy jolted, reining in his big sorrel, who alone was in condition to keep on going at full speed. "No use. Let them go."

"Heading north by west!" Cameron growled, shaking his fist at the vanishing riders. "Uh-huh, they're heading for Tascosa, sure as shooting. Some of Basset Shaw's hellions, all right. What we ought to do is ride up there and gut-shoot *him*."

"Take care of that later," Hardy answered briefly. "First, who's hurt and how bad? 'Pears everybody has managed to stay in his hull, so it can't be too bad."

The man with the bullet-gashed cheek profanely refused assistance. He had already tied his neckerchief around the wound.

"Nothing to it," he declared. "Bleeding's

about stopped already. It'll just make me look even purtier than before. Take a look at Russell."

The punctured arm was a bit more serious, but with one neckerchief for a bandage and a second for a sling, Russell insisted he'd make out, and like the other rugged cowhand made light of his hurt.

These matters attended to, they rode back to the belt of chaparral, slowing their horses and shouting reassurance to the teamsters as they neared the growth. Bellows of relief answered them, and there was a flickering of improvised torches on the far side of the brush.

"You got two of the sidewinders, Boss," an excited wagoneer told Hardy as he reined in beside the wagons. "One all shot to pieces and the other drilled dead center. Nope, none of us fellers ever saw 'em before. Mean-looking cusses."

None of the guards recognized the dead drygulchers, either.

"Load 'em on one of the wagons and we'll take them to town," Hardy decided. "No sense in making the sheriff ride clear out here to look over such scum. Pity we didn't get their horses; brands might have told us something."

"They hightailed with the rest," Cameron remarked.

"We found a whopping big bundle of oily rags and junk," one of the teamsters interposed. "Guess they figured to burn the wagons."

"Reckon that was the general idea," Hardy agreed. "Well, let's get moving; we're going to be late for supper."

Sheriff Nance swore in weary disgust when Hardy reported the latest outrage.

"Why did you have to squat in this section!" he complained querulously. "You and your bone pickin'! Everything was peaceful till you came along."

"Would suit me fine if it had stayed peaceful, but some other folks appear to have different ideas," Hardy answered.

The sheriff swore some more. "I could track you anywhere by just following the trail of bodies," he grumbled. "And you couldn't identify any of those hellions if you saw them again?"

"It was almost pitch dark when we got close enough to have a look at them, and the light from that burning waste didn't help; it just dazzled our eyes," Hardy explained. "If it hadn't been for that, I've a notion we might have accounted for some more of them; it was blind shooting. Lucky for us we were back in the shadow, which gave us a bit of advantage. But if we hadn't caught sight of them from up on that slope, they would have gotten away with it and the wagons would have gone up in smoke."

"The whole thing doesn't seem to make sense," puzzled the sheriff. "Taking chances on a bad shooting just to burn a few wagons seems like a plumb senseless thing to do."

"Maybe not so senseless when you take into consideration the fact that I made a short-time bank loan, with my holdings as security, to get the money I needed to pay for the last section of land I bought and to stock my range," Hardy pointed out. "If I'd lost those wagons I'd have been held up for weeks, maybe longer, in my bone picking; and getting the money I need depends on cleaning out that cache of bones in the canyon, and no time to waste."

"Still doesn't seem to make sense," said the sheriff. "Reckon you wouldn't have had any trouble getting the bank to give you an extension, your circumstances being what they are."

"I've thought of that," admitted Hardy, "and it's got me puzzled a bit. Well, it doesn't matter now. Their little scheme slipped up and I'll see to it they don't get another chance. Suppose you'll hold an inquest tomorrow?"

"Oh, I suppose so," conceded the sheriff, "and let folks have a look at those sidewinders, though I'll bet money nobody remembers ever seeing them before. Then we'll plant 'em. Thanks to you, we're getting a pretty nice Boot Hill started. If this keeps up, ours will soon be ahead of the one they're so proud of up at Tascosa."

"We ought to send the pair we got to Tascosa," growled Tom Cameron. "That's where they came from."

"You've got no proof of that, Cameron," Sheriff Nance objected sharply.

"No, I admit I got no proof," Cameron replied, "but when we first saw 'em they were coming from that direction, and the ones that got away headed back in that direction. If I had my way I'd ride up there and gut-shoot Basset Shaw on general principles."

"Wouldn't be good judgment," said Nance. "Not that I'd bother my head about it. Tascosa is in Oldham County, and I've got no authority over there, for which I'm duly thankful. Potter is bad enough, but Oldham, gentlemen, hush! Take my advice, both of you, and stay away from there."

Neither argued the point.

CHAPTER VII

The guards and teamsters celebrated their adventure in a respectable manner by getting drunk. Hardy and Cameron had a few drinks on their own account and went to bed.

Sheriff Nance was right: nobody could recall seeing the two dead men.

"Brought in from New Mexico or some place to do the job," was the general concensus of opinion.

The next day the bone pickers, little perturbed by their experience, went back to work, and within a few weeks the canyon was cleaned out without further disturbance.

The haul was not as big as Hardy had hoped it would be, but he figured he had enough money to get by. And although the wagons would now have to range far and wide over the prairie for their loads, there were still plenty of bones to be gathered.

With the wagons scattered all over the section, Hardy felt there was little danger that they would be molested. Nothing worth while was to be gained from drygulching a lone wagon, with the drivers and pickers armed and ready to fight back. So he decided his troop of guards was no longer necessary. He called them together for a talk.

"Guess your chore is finished," he told them. " 'Bout time for you to take on something else."

"Uh-huh, reckon we'll have to do a little chuck line riding," agreed big Bill Jasper.

"Not unless you're in the mood for it," replied Hardy. Tom Cameron, who knew what was coming, had difficulty hiding a grin.

"Reckon it ain't a matter of being in the mood for it; we ain't got much choice," said Jasper. "Jobs of riding ain't over easy to come by in this section right now."

"So I figure, and because of it, I guess the best thing you can do is stay on with me," Hardy said, sober as a judge.

"Now what in tarnation do you mean by that?" asked the bewildered Jasper.

"Bill," Hardy returned, "you'll remember when I hired you jiggers, one of the questions I asked was, were you or had you been cowhands? Remember?"

"Uh-huh, guess that's so," Jasper admitted.

"Well," said Hardy, "when I hired you as guards I figured I might as well hire me some cowhands while I was at it; it would give me a good chance to size them up, too. So if it's agreeable with you gents, you'll quit being bone picker guards and get ready to start chambermaiding cows for the Four Sixes Ranch. You see, I got my start in a poker game with four sixes against an ace-full, so I figured 6666 would be just about the right brand for my cows; I've already registered it. First we'll get busy and build a ranchhouse, a better bunkhouse and the other shacks we'll need; then we'll proceed to get some cows."

For a moment there was a astonished silence; then a wild whoop went up and Hardy was very nearly bowled over by slaps on the back.

"Sure figure it was my lucky day when I signed up with you, Boss," chuckled Jasper, "and I reckon that goes for the rest of the boys."

"That's what we'll try and make it, a lucky day for all of us," Hardy told him.

Leaving the building chore to Tom Cameron, who was thoroughly competent in such matters, Hardy set out to pay Colonel Goodnight a visit.

As he rode south by east across the prairie, Cliff Hardy marvelled at the remarkable flat country spread before his eyes.

Finally, however, he came to a break in the flatness, that strange and wonderful cleft across the Panhandle Plains of Texas known as the Palo Duro Canyon.

Colonel Charles Goodnight, the first man to run cows onto the Staked Plains, had been caught in the panic of 1873. He had salvaged out of the wreck of his property eighteen hundred longhorns. These he drove from his Colorado ranch to the Palo Duro. With his covered wagons, his herd, his family and his cowhands, he made camp. He had followed an old Indian trail which led into the Palo Duro over the Cap Rock. The wagons had to be unloaded, taken to pieces and, along with provisions and household goods, lowered by ropes to the valley below by way of a rock slide. Near the mouth of the canyon, which was miles wide and very deep, an ideal cattle range fenced in with walls hundreds of feet high, Goodnight first lived in a dugout, the beginning of the great JA Ranch. . . .

Colonel Goodnight received his former cowhand hospitably. He had always rather liked Cliff Hardy despite his quick temper that was prone to get him into trouble.

"Been watching your progress, son, and I'm pleased to see you getting along so well," the colonel said. "I always though you had it in you if you could just get over your darn shiftlessness and control your temper a bit. Anything I can do for you?"

"I'd like to ask you a question or two, sir," Hardy replied.

"Shoot," said the colonel.

"About that Hereford stock you brought in to breed with your longhorns, sir, I believe you got them in Oklahoma?"

"That's right," replied Goodnight. "I bought them from Silas Releford, who has a place just this side of Erick in Beckham County. Hauled 'em over here in wagons."

Hardy nodded, his eyes thoughtful. "Think I could make a deal with Releford, say for about five hundred head?" he asked.

The veteran cattleman stared. "Sure you could make a deal with Si," he answered. "Selling stock, mostly improved stuff for breeding purposes, is his business, and I expect at this time of the year he'd have five hundred to turn loose. But I'd like you to tell me how in the devil you figure to get together enough wagons to haul five hundred head all the way from Oklahoma over here?"

"Don't figure to haul them," Hardy replied. "I aim to drive them here."

Colonel Goodnight shook his head. "Son, you can't do it," he declared. "Those cows are heavy and fat and the horn of their hoofs is soft and spongy. You never could drive them over the rough country between here and there. They'd be all stove up and go lame on you in no time."

"I've got a notion how it can be done," Hardy replied cheerfully.

The rancher shook his head again and looked expectant, but Hardy only grinned.

"When I see it I'll believe it," said the colonel.

"And how about making a deal with you, sir, after I get back, say for five hundred long-horns?" Hardy asked.

"Reckon we can get together," agreed Goodnight. "Five hundred cows will make a very nice herd to start with. I wasn't so terribly much better off when I started here."

"A thousand I'll start with," Hardy corrected, with another grin.

The grin was infectious, and the colonel had to chuckle. "Okay, when I see it I'll believe it," he said.

Hardy spent the night at the JA ranchhouse, and after a hearty breakfast and a cordial good-bye from the colonel he rode east.

He took his time and covered the hundred and twenty miles in three days. Nearing Erick across the Oklahoma line, he had no difficulty in locating the Walking R Ranch owned by Silas Releford.

The old cattleman received him hospitably and was ready to talk business.

"Sure I can let you have five hundred head," he agreed. "The very best stuff, too, even better than what I sold Goodnight."

He hesitated, tugged his mustache, then voiced the same warning as had Colonel Goodnight.

"But, son, although I don't like to lose a good deal, I'm not much on taking advantage of somebody's ignorance," he said. "You can't never run those cows from here to the Panhandle. They'll go lame on you before you've covered half the distance. You'll be lucky if you get fifty head through."

"I believe I can do it," Hardy replied. "Suppose there's a blacksmith shop around here, isn't there?"

"Sure," replied Releford. "Two good ones at Erick, one just as you enter the town from over here."

"And I reckon I can buy horseshoes in Erick?"

"All you want," said Releford. "What's the matter—your horse cast an iron?"

"Nope, he's got all four of 'em right where they belong," Hardy answered. "Now about the price of that stock—figure it up, will you?"

Releford did the figuring, and insisted Hardy check on it. Hardy paid him for the herd.

"Glad to get rid of all that cash," he said with a grin. "Now you can worry about it."

"And *you* can worry about how you're going to get those cows to the Panhandle," said Releford as he pocketed the big bills. "When will you come for them?"

"Should be back in about ten days or so," Hardy told him.

Leaving the cattleman, Hardy rode into town and had a talk with the blacksmith.

"Sounds loco to me, but maybe it ain't after all," said that worthy. "Well, I'll have everything ready for you when you get back. Yes, I can arrange for the irons. So long."

As Hardy rode away, the bearded smith turned to his helper.

"There goes either the biggest fool or one of the smartest jiggers that ever rode out of Texas," he stated with emphasis, adding thoughtfully, "and I'm darned if I'm sure which."

When he got back to the Four Sixes, Hardy found the construction work going smoothly. However, he at once ordered the building operations discontinued for the time being. He bought a chuck wagon and hired a cook of an astounding irascibility of disposition and outstanding culinary ability. Two days after his arrival, the whole Four Sixes outfit rolled east and reached Silas Releford's ranch without mishap. Hardy put his novel scheme into practice.

The blacksmith had been as good as his word and had everything in readiness. The Four Sixes punchers sweated and swore, and nailed iron shoes to the hoofs of the five hundred head of cattle Hardy had purchased from Releford. The slow, heavy and amiable beasts regarded the procedure with mild astonishment but offered no serious objections to the innovation.

Erick and its environs buzzed with discussion and argument. Some folks were inclined to laugh and brand Hardy as loco as a herder full of sheep dip. Others, however, took a more serious view of the matter.

"That young squirt may have something," declared a crusty old-timer who had been around considerable and whose opinions were listened to with respect. "If irons keep a horse's hoofs from getting split and stove up, why not a cow's? Yes, he may have something."

Old Silas Releford was dubious but interested, "Well, son, if it works, I've a notion you've started something," he told Hardy. "And you know, it *may* work. Let me know after you get back to the Panhandle. By the way, ain't you the feller who started the bone picking around Ragtown?"

Hardy admitted that he was.

Releford nodded his head sagely. "And I reckon folks laughed when you rolled in with your first wagonload; but it wasn't long till they were laughing out of the other side of their faces. May happen again. And as old Beasley said, if this fool notion works, you sure have started something."

CHAPTER VIII

Finally all was in readiness, and early one morning the big herd rolled westward, the heavy placid animals moving forward sturdily, apparently not in the least inconvenienced by their unaccustomed foot gear. Tom Cameron closely watched their progress over the rough and stony ground west of the Walking R holdings and grew enthusiastic.

"Boss," he said, "I believe you've made a ten strike. Those rocks don't bother 'em a bit, and this would be hard going even for longhorns. Yes, by God! I believe it's going to work. But I wish we had 'em all safe on our spread. We got some bad country to cross, and a herd like this would make a wide-looper's mouth water."

Hardy was of the same opinion; and more than the possibility of a chance raid by some rustling outfit hanging out in the hills bothered him. It was common knowledge around Amarillo that he intended to drive a herd back from Oklahoma, and he hadn't forgotten the raid on his bone wagons. If he lost the herd he would be financially crippled and unable to meet his bank note when it fell due.

The possibility that a rustling bunch would tackle a herd guarded by a dozen armed men was rather remote, but there were always ways of doing things that discounted odds. If, as Hardy suspected, Basset Shaw was the troublemaker who was seeking to cause him to lose his holdings, almost anything was possible. Shaw was a shrewd and unscrupulous operator, if what he had been able to learn of the man was true, and he had no reason to believe it wasn't. And ahead was the wild and rugged region of the "Cap Rock," once a favorite haunt of the Comanches, where conditions were ideal for a quick and deadly raid on a passing herd.

Although the tractable improved stock was much easier to handle than rambunctious longhorns, the traditional procedure of handling a herd on the trail was followed.

Nobody rode directly in front of the herd. Riding off to the side and near the head of the column were the point men who guided the herd. When the point or lead men wished to change the direction of the herd they would ride abreast of the lead cattle. One would veer away from the herd; the other would crowd toward it. The cows would slant away from the approaching horseman and toward the one that was drawing away. Hardy placed picked men at this post of greatest responsibility.

About a third of the way back from the point men were the swing riders, whose post was where the herd would begin to bend in case of a change of course. Another third of the way back were the flank riders. It was their duty, in which they were assisted by the swing riders, to block any wandering to the side and to drive off any foreign cattle that might seek to join the trail herd.

Behind the herd, cursing the dust and the laggards, were the drag riders who had to prod along the lazy and obstinate beeves. This was a disagreeable chore, but one entailing great responsibility, especially in wild country where there was danger of an attack by rustlers. Tom Cameron commanded the drag riders.

Cliff Hardy took upon himself the chore of trail boss. It was his duty, in addition to keeping an eye on everything, to ride ahead and search out watering places and good grazing ground where the herd could bed down for the night.

Circumstances being what they were, he took Cameron with him when he rode on ahead, toward the middle of the afternoon.

Rolling along behind the drag was the chuck wagon piloted by the cook, and a remuda of spare horses attended by a mounted hand. In the afternoon the chuck wagon would roll ahead and take the lead, so that the cook could set up business where Hardy designated a bedding down ground and have supper ready by the time the herd was bedded down.

By mid-morning of the third day out they were in the Cap Rock region, following a branch of that old and bitter trail which led to the "Valley of Tears."

It was a trail of blood and sorrow, but the cowhands gave little thought to its dark history although very much alert to the possibilities of raid or ambush. However, the day and the night passed without incident.

Hardy was a bit anxious about the inhospitable terrain when he and Cameron rode ahead the next afternoon; there was no water and forage was practically nonexistent.

"But if I'm figuring right, a good day's march should bring us to a canyon mouth where there's grass and a creek," he told the range boss. "Anyhow, we'll just have to keep rolling till we reach the place. I rode through here on my way back from Erick, and till we get to that canyon there isn't a drop of water, to say nothing of grass."

Hardy breathed a sigh of relief when they finally reached the spot for which he was searching.

"Better than I expected," he said. "They should make it here with the cows by sundown."

The canyon mouth, which was fairly wide, was grassy. It narrowed rapidly, however, and was soon choked by a thick, tall stand of chaparral growth. Along one sloping wall ran a shallow little stream that crossed the trail and tumbled down a gentle slope which, about half a mile farther on, ended in what was apparently a second and narrower canyon.

Hardy and Cameron rode up the gorge a little way and dismounted to let their horses drink. Hardy began rolling a cigarette, his gaze absently resting on the clear water.

Suddenly his fingers stopped moving and his gaze became fixed on an object bobbing along on the surface.

"Tom," he exclaimed, "do you see that?"

Cameron peered with puckered lids. "It's only a cork," he replied.

"Yes, only a cork," Hardy repeated grimly. "But will you tell me what a cork is doing floating in the water up here in the Cap Rock?"

"Reckon somebody must have dropped it in the creek," Cameron guessed.

"Exactly," Hardy agreed. "Somebody dropped it in the creek—somebody farther up the canyon. And what legitimate business would anybody have up there, I'd like to know?"

Cameron looked startled. "You mean somebody is there, holed up in the brush?"

"Well, that cork didn't drop from a tree," Hardy returned.

"Shall we ride up and see?" Cameron suggested.

"And very likely lean against the hot end of a passing slug, if somebody is up there," Hardy replied. "Wait; this will take some thinking out."

He was silent for some moments; then:

"Tom, we've got to bed down here," he said. "There's no more water between here and the Plains, and no grass; and we can't make a night drive over the country ahead. I believe I've got the thing figured out. If I'm right about it, everything should be okay. If I'm wrong, and there's a chance I can be wrong, and we go through with it, we'll very likely be dead right after dark. It's a gamble, and I'm going to put it up to you. If you're willing to take the chance and figure it will be okay with the boys, we'll go through with it. We can't tell the boys right off what we plan to do. If we tell them, it's almost certain to give the whole scheme away, if those hellions up there are keeping a watch on us."

"Shoot," said Cameron. "Don't worry about the boys. Anything you and I decide will be okay with them. Let's have it."

"As I figure it," Hardy said slowly, "if there is someone holed up in the canyon waiting to take a whack at us, they're most likely not to move until some time after dark, after we've settled down for the night. According to my way of thinking, that would be the logical way for them to work it, with the advantages all on their side, especially if they have no reason to think we've gotten suspicious. We'll bed down here and let them think we don't suspect a thing; then we'll try and arrange things to turn the tables on those gents with larceny in mind. But as I said, if I'm wrong—well—" There was no need to finish the sentence.

Cameron shrugged his big shoulders. "If you don't gamble you can't win," he commented. "Twirl your loop, feller; I'll be with you on the drag!"

"We won't tell the boys what we suspect till the last minute when we're all ready to line things up," Hardy went on. "Let them get the least bit jumpy and start looking up the canyon and they'll give the whole thing away. It'll be up to you and me to keep a sharp watch on that brush without appearing to do so and to be ready to go into action at the first sign that something's not right."

"We'll work it," said Cameron. "What'll we do now?"

"Start a fire and loaf around till the chuck wagon shows," Hardy decided. "That's what we're expected to do. Build the fire over at the base of the far slope. You'll notice that slope is pretty well brush-grown; it's be just right for what I have in mind."

Getting the rigs off their horses and turning them loose to graze, they went about the chore of getting the camp ready, apparently intent only on what they were doing but keeping a sharp watch on the bristle of dark and silent growth that choked the canyon only a few hundred yards from its mouth. It was a risky business, moving about the open clearing, not knowing from one minute to the next if gun barrels might be lined in their direction.

However, nothing happened. The chuck wagon, driven by the vituperative cook, rolled down the trail and came to a halt not far from

the fire. The cook began hauling out his pans
and pots and Dutch ovens. Another hour and
the bleating of the approaching herd was audi-
ble. It was already sunset, and the brush up the
canyon was swatched in shadows that slowly
crept over the grass below to purple the waters
of the stream and beat futilely against the glow
of the fire.

The cowboys ate their simple meal beside the
fire, rolled cigarettes and smoked contentedly.
The cattle grazed, spreading over the rich grass-
land of the canyon mouth. Gradually they drew
together; soon they would bunch, chew their
cuds for a while and then lie down, rumbling
and grunting. About midnight, as if by a prearranged signal, they would all get up, turn
around and lie down on the other side. There
was no danger of them straying away from the
grass and water, and it was not necessary to set
a night guard. The horses had been hobbled a
little distance down the canyon from the fire, all
except Rojo, Hardy's great sorrel, who was allowed to roam at will. Hardy knew he would
take care of himself and always come at his
master's whistle.

The fire was allowed to die down, for the
night was warm. When it was little more than
a flicker that cast vague and elusive shadows,

Hardy gathered the hands together and told them what he figured was in the wind. The information was greeted with muttered curses. Apprehensive glances were sent toward the black stand of brush up the canyon, barely visible in the glimmer cast by the stars and a thick rind of moon that lazed near the zenith.

"So roll your blankets and place them around the fire, just like you were sleeping in them," Hardy concluded. "Then slide up the slope into the brush and hole up. Careful, now, not to make a noise. If the hellions are really back in the chaparral, they may have moved in closer after it got dark. Take it easy and see that your guns are in working order. If they do make a try, I figure it'll be just about an hour or two from now, when they figure everybody will be asleep. Let's go!"

The maneuver was executed in perfect silence. The rolled blankets looked enough like sleeping men to deceive anyone except on a close inspection. From where he lounged comfortably beneath a bush, Hardy could almost believe it was a dozen punchers industriously pounding their ears.

Gradually the cattle bunched and lay down. The moon worked its way across the sky, its beams slanting into the canyon mouth. The little stream purled and rippled. Otherwise, aside from the small noises made by the sleepy cows, the night was deathly still. From the far distance came the wild, hauntingly beautiful call of a hunting wolf. An owl on some blasted tree whined a querulous answer. Somewhere a coyote yipped peevishly. Then all was still save for a faint rustling of the leaves as a lonely little wind wandered about, wondering where to go.

It was Cliff Hardy's keen ears that caught the faint jingle of a bit iron somewhere up the canyon. He squeezed Tom Cameron's arm.

"They're there all right," he whispered. "Easy, now, and don't make a move till I give the word. We want to hit them where it hurts most."

Tense, alert, their nerves tightened to the breaking point with strain, their palms sweating, the Four Sixes hands watched and waited. Abruptly there was another sound from the growth, a soft, insistent sound, as if a giant were gently pressing aside the branches with his hands. Then darker shadows loomed against the gray-black block of the brush; shadows that drifted down the canyon, the horses' hoofs making but a whisper of sound on the heavy grass.

Another moment of crawling suspense; then a thud of irons beat on the ground. The canyon walls rocked to a roar of gunfire. The blanket rolls beside the nearly dead fire twiched and jerked as bullets hammered them. Again and again the outlaws poured lead into what they thought to be the unprepared camp.

"The cold-blooded snakes!" Tom Cameron breathed.

Confident that they had nothing more to fear from the occupants of the blankets, the rustlers charged toward the herd, shooting and yelling, and got a surprise. Old mossyback longhorns would already have been in full flight from the canyon, but the placid improved stock did not stampede. The startled, bewildered cows merely milled and bellowed and clumped closer and closer together.

Swearing exasperated oaths, the wideloopers, bunched together, sent their horses directly at the herd, slickers snapping and crackling. And the storm blast of death struck them.

At Hardy's word of command, the cowboys opened fire. The moon was well down the western sky now, and the shadows were thickening in the canyon; it was poor shooting light. But just the same that first concentrated hail of lead emptied four saddles. The remaining outlaws, with howls of terror, scattered in all directions and fled madly toward the trail. Another fell as the hands continued to fire as fast as they could pull trigger. Cliff Hardy, using his Winchester, lined sights with the rearmost horseman. The rifle cracked; the man slumped from his hull like a sack of old clothes; the riderless horse, stirrups flapping wildly, saddle leather popping, dashed on after its fellows. The beat of fast hoofs died away in the west.

"Well, reckon that's about all," Hardy said quietly. "Let's go see how many scalps we collected."

"I wish we'd done for the whole bunch of 'em!" growled big Bill Jasper. "Did you ever see anything so cold-blooded as the way they shot up those blanket rolls? They figured to murder every last one of us!"

"That was the general idea, I guess," Hardy agreed.

"And if it hadn't been for you spotting that cork this afternoon and figuring out what it meant, they'd have gotten away with it," declared Cameron. "That was smart thinking, Boss, almighty smart thinking."

"Seems it paid off, anyhow," Hardy replied. "Let's go."

Lanterns were lighted and the bodies were examined. They were hard-looking specimens, but with nothing to distinguish them from the general run of their kind. Their pockets revealed nothing of importance save a rather large amount of money.

"Divide it up among the boys," Hardy told Cameron. "They've got something coming for all the sleep they lost."

"What shall we do with the bodies—pack 'em in to the sheriff?" Cameron asked.

"We're not in Potter County," Hardy answered. "Sheriff Nance has no authority over here. Fact is, I'm not sure what county we are in. It would just be a waste of time hunting up somebody to take charge of them. There are a couple of spades in the chuck wagon, I believe; tomorrow morning before we pull out we'll dig a hole and dump 'em in."

"I'd say to leave 'em lay here, only I ain't got nothing against the buzzards and wouldn't want to see them pizened," growled Jasper.

"Anyway, it looks like we did for more than half of the bushwackers," observed Cameron. "I don't think there was more than ten or eleven in the bunch."

"About right, I'd say," agreed Hardy. "Well, the cows appear to have quieted down, and we might as well go to bed. Don't think there'll be any more excitement tonight."

"Not from those hellions," chuckled Cameron. "They went away from here so fast you could hear them whizz!"

CHAPTER IX

The herd made good time the next day, and by afternoon they were free of the ominous Cap Rock and well out on the sunny plains, where they found water and made a comfortable camp.

"And not a cow lamed or stove up," said Cameron. "Boss, your idea sure paid off."

That was what Colonel Goodnight thought when Hardy bedded his cows at the mouth of the Palo Duro and visited the JA owner. He repeated the very words old Silas Releford had used.

"Hardy," he said, "I believe you've started something. Why nobody ever thought of it before is beyond me. About the longhorns you want—you can have 'em, and at a bargain. I figure what you've taught me about moving stock is worth considerable. I'll have them rounded up tomorrow, and you can run them along with your Herefords. And that's a fine-looking bunch of stock you've got. Releford must have taken a shine to you. Yes, sir, fine stuff."

The remainder of the drive to the Four Sixes was made without incident. Work was resumed on the buildings, waterholes were dug and fed from the stream by means of ditches. Cliff Hardy was in business.

Since things were moving along in a satisfactory manner, Hardy visited the bank that held his note. It wasn't due for another week, but the bone picking business had been going well and he had the money to pay it off. He wanted to take care of the matter without delay and get it off his hands. But when he approached the banker, he got a surprise.

"Ah, yes, the mortgage," said the banker. "Well, Hardy, the bank doesn't own that note any longer. We sold it a couple of months ago."

"The devil you did!" Hardy exclaimed. "Why wasn't I notified?"

"Such a note," the banker explained, "is negotiable property and can be bought, sold or transferred, and it is not required that the mortgagor be notified of the transaction, although," he added, "as a matter of courtesy we would have done so before the note falls due."

"I see," Hardy said. "And who did you sell it to?"

"We sold it to Mr. Basset Shaw of Tascosa," replied the banker.

Hardy stared at him. "Basset Shaw!" he repeated.

"That's right," said the banker. "Mr. Shaw deals in such things; I understand he owns quite a few, here and elsewhere. They're usually a good investment."

"No doubt, sometimes," Hardy agreed dryly. "So I suppose I'll have to take the matter up with Basset Shaw."

"That's right," repeated the banker. "However, I suppose if you desire to pay off the note, it could be arranged for the bank to handle the payment so you wouldn't have to go to the trouble of seeing Shaw."

"I think I'll pay him personally," Hardy said. "Much obliged for the offer, though."

"Don't mention it," said the banker, "and any time we can do something for you, don't hesitate to ask. We feel that you are an up and coming young man in this section and will be pleased to have you deal with us."

"Up and coming, or going," Hardy replied with a smile that puzzled the banker.

When Hardy left the bank he headed straight for a saloon across the street. He needed a drink, and a little time to get control of himself. His anger was at a white heat, and for the moment he was incapable of coherent thought.

After a couple of slugs of straight whiskey and a third to sip, he cooled down a little, his taut nerves relaxed, and he was able to review the situation in a rational manner.

Shaw's scheme was devilish in its simplicity. Make it impossible for Hardy to meet the note, refuse an extension and foreclose. If the raid on his wagon train had been successful, that would have been fairly easy. If the wideloopers had succeeded in their attack, he, Hardy, would have been dead and the ultimate result would have been the same. It appeared that Shaw would stop at nothing to achieve his ends. And the most aggravating part of the whole affair was the fact that though he was convinced in his own mind that Basset Shaw was the prime mover in the business, he had not one iota of proof that he was. Just the same, Hardy promised himself a showdown with the schemer. Perhaps a little man-to-man encounter would get results; anyhow, he was going to try it.

The next morning at sunrise, Hardy set out for Tascosa. He rode almost due west until he reached a point locally known as "The Meadow," later to be the site of Vega, the county seat of Oldham County. Then he turned north, following a well travelled trail. Mid-afternoon found his horse's hoofs thudding on the boards of the old wooden bridge that spanned the Canadian, on the north bank of which was Tascosa, "The Cowboy Capital of the Plains."

Passing the sprawling lumber yards, Hardy followed Bridge Street and turned east on Main. Basset Shaw's saloon, he knew, was on Main Street near the corner of Main and McMasters. In front of the broad plate glass window, he dropped the split reins to the ground beside a hitch rack and entered the saloon, which was fairly busy, although the hour was still early. A bartender nodded a cordial greeting.

"I'd like to see Basset Shaw," Hardy told him.

"Reckon you'll find him over at his house about now," the barkeep replied. "It's at the corner of Spring Street and Maybry Avenue. Spring Street's the next street west of here. Maybry is the next corner after Court Street, the first street you cross going north."

Hardy thanked the drink juggler and, after following directions, soon pulled up in front of a comfortable-looking house with trees growing in the yard. He dismounted and walked toward the veranda. As he drew near he saw the veranda had an occupant, a girl.

She was a very pretty girl, Hardy thought. She was small and slender, with astonishingly big blue eyes, curly dark hair and vivid red lips, a trifle full but sweetly turned. He absently noted that there were a few freckles delicately powdering the bridge of her straight little nose. Her complexion was creamily golden, with a touch of color in each cheek.

"Hello," she said as he paused at the foot of the steps.

"I was told Basset Shaw is here, and I'd like to see him," Hardy replied, removing his hat.

"He's back in the dining room having something to eat," the girl replied. "I'll take you to him, Mr.—" She paused expectantly.

Hardy supplied his name. She nodded brightly. "Come in, Mr. Hardy," she invited. "Mr. Shaw is my uncle; I'm Rita Sostenes."

Hardy's eyes widened a little as she pronounced the name. Her own eyes danced and there was the suspicion of a dimple at one corner of her red mouth.

"Oh, you don't have to look startled, although everybody does, it seems," she said. "My grandfather *was* Sostenes l'Archevêque, the bandit leader, but his son, my father, was a respectable trader and raiser of sheep and a friend of Colonel Charles Goodnight. He married Uncle

Basset's sister. They're both dead now, and I live with Uncle Basset."

"I see," Hardy said a bit dazedly.

"You don't, but it doesn't matter," she replied. "Come on; I'll take you in to Uncle Basset."

Hardy followed her. He was surprised to see how tiny she was when she stood up, but her figure was well nigh perfect, and she walked with a grace that was bound to quicken the pulses of any normal young man.

She led the way down a long hall, ushered him into a room, and there, seated at a large table spread with a snowy cloth and sipping a cup of very hot coffee, was Basset Shaw. He nodded to Hardy and continued to sip coffee.

Hardy, who had paused just inside the door, felt his anger surge, but the burning words of denunciation he had so carefully rehearsed for Basset Shaw's benefit remained unspoken. It is difficult to denounce a man who insists upon drinking coffee. Besides, the girl was speaking.

"Uncle Basset, this is Mr. Cliff Hardy who says he wants to see you," she said.

"We've met before," said Shaw, the steaming cup still at his lips. "Sit down, Hardy. Rita, tell the cook to bring him something to eat. He used to be a cowhand, and cowhands are always hungry."

"Sit down, Mr. Hardy, please do," added Rita, pulling out a chair.

Hardy sat down, and attacked the really excellent dinner with a ferocity that should have been exercised against Shaw.

Rita, who apparently had already eaten or wasn't hungry, drew a chair back from the table, sat down and crossed her very pretty ankles. Perhaps sensing that there was tension between the two men, she chatted gaily about various things, including rangeland matters, asking Hardy questions that showed a surprising knowledge of the cattle business. Hardy answered in monosyllables—he was still trying to get his badly disordered faculties into something like coherent shape. Basset Shaw lived up to his nickname of "Silent" Shaw and said little, speaking only when Rita asked him a direct question.

As he ate, Hardy studied the man opposite him. He was, he thought, typical of the successful and ofttimes ruthless frontiersmen he had met. He was tall, finely formed, with a square, rugged, impassive face. His skin had a healthy outdoor look; his mouth was tight-lipped, intolerant.

What set him apart, Hardy felt, was his eyes. They were large and almost as deeply blue as

Rita's; but they had a peculiar quality of lighting up when he spoke, and becoming expressionless again when he was silent. And when that strange gleam lighted them, they became purplish in color. Hardy had a feeling that in the dark they would glow like a cat's. They had a peculiar, disquieting effect.

Finally Hardy finished eating and pushed back his plate. Shaw was smoking a cigar. Rita took the cue to excuse herself and leave the room.

The purplish gleam was in Basset Shaw's eyes as he fixed them on Hardy, who met his gaze unflinchingly.

"Suppose you've come to talk about the mortgage," he said.

"That's right," Hardy replied. "Or rather, I've come to pay it off." He drew a thick packet of bills from his pocket as he spoke and laid them on the table.

Shaw made no move to take the money. He puffed on his cigar.

"Hardy," he said, "I'm in the habit of getting whatever I go after."

"So I've been given to understand," Hardy answered. Shaw nodded his head.

"I think," he said, "it would be better for you to keep that money and let me foreclose, after

I have adequately recompensed you for your time and trouble."

"I think not," Hardy replied tartly.

"It might be safer," Shaw observed.

Hardy felt his anger mounting again, but he controlled it. He laid his forearm on the table and leaned forward a little.

"Shaw," he said, "the very last thing I ever wanted to be was a killer; but because of you, I'm pretty well on the way to becoming one. I think four, possibly five, is the number right now. And when a man starts killing, it get progressively easier, as I have good reason to know. After two or three, you get so you don't mind. Don't forget that, Shaw. Don't forget it!"

"I won't," Shaw replied. "Have a cigar."

Not to be outdone, Hardy accepted the cigar. Shaw picked up the packet of bills, and without counting them stuffed them in his pocket. "I'll get your note," he said, and walked out. He returned a few minutes later with the paper and handed it to Hardy. He regarded him quizzically.

"Any time you happen to be in town, drop in at my place for a drink on the house," he said. "And remember, when you're under my roof, you're my guest. Understand?"

Hardy understood perfectly. When partaking

of Basset Shaw's hospitality, he was inviolate; it was the code of the Frontier, respected even by the outlaw fraternity and the coldest killers. Suddenly he grinned.

"Shaw," he said, "I'm liable to take you up on it."

"On what?" Shaw asked, looking a trifle puzzled and a bit suspicious.

"On being your guest," Hardy replied. He rose to his feet and left the room. Basset Shaw gazed after him, the purplish gleam bright in his eyes.

CHAPTER X

Rita was on the veranda when Hardy walked through the front door. She smiled up at him.

"All through?" she asked.

"Yes, all through with business," Hardy replied. He sat down on the front step, turned to face her and began rolling a cigarette, after tossing the half smoked cigar aside. He cocked his eye upward.

"I see this porch has a roof," he remarked.

"Why, yes, it has," she agreed. "What of it?"

"Handy things," Hardy commented. "Keep away the rain."

Rita gave him a slightly exasperated glance.

"If that's just a labored effort to make conversation, it really isn't necessary," she said. "I can talk enough for both of us."

"I'm a mighty good listener," Hardy declared.

"All right," she said. "I'll talk about something in which a man is always greatly interested."

"What's that?"

"Himself! I didn't catch the significance of your name at first, but later it came to me. I recently read quite an article about you in Tascosa's newspaper, *The Pioneer*. You're the man they call the Bone Picker, aren't you?"

"I have been called that," Hardy admitted.

"And by picking bones you earned enough money to buy a big ranch."

"Oh, it's not big, as spreads hereabouts go," Hardy replied, "but it is a pretty good holding."

"And only two years ago you were just a cowhand, working for wages. How in the world did you do it?"

"By getting drunk," Hardy returned cheerfully. She gave him another exasperated glance.

"It seems," she said, "that it is a habit with you to speak in riddles. Now just what do you mean by that statement?"

Hardy told her humorously of the all-night poker game and his rambling drive across the prairie at the back of a six-horse team. She laughed at first, then grew serious.

"But you weren't drunk when you figured out what bone picking could mean, something it appears nobody else had thought of."

"Nope, guess I wasn't," Hardy admitted.

"What a marvelous success story!" she exclaimed. "It sounds like something from a book. I'm beginning to think, Mr. Hardy, that you are an unusual man. And are you trying to interest my uncle in bone picking?"

"I've a notion he's already interested in picking bones," Hardy replied with a grim significance that was lost on her.

"He has many interests," she said thoughtfully. "He seems to be obsessed with an overwhelming ambition to get on top; but I wonder if the sweaty climb is really worth while. I sometimes feel that one can find a greater contentment in a moderate success."

Hardy's interest in her quickened. He had thought of her only as a very pretty girl, and pretty girls always interested Cliff Hardy; but her remarks seemed to indicate an intelligence that was unusual.

"And what is your definition of a moderate success?" he asked.

"To acquire enough to live comfortably and be in a position to lend a helping hand to those who need it," she replied quickly.

"That sounds sensible," Hardy admitted.

"And what is your ambition?" she asked.

"To own a cow factory and make it pay."

Hardy chuckled. "Have to admit I haven't thought beyond that."

"And I think you'll be happier if you don't think any farther," she said. "I'll have to go; my uncle is calling me."

"May I see you again?" he asked as he stood up.

"If you wish," she replied. "You'll always be welcome."

"Okay, we'll let it go at that." He smiled. "Goodbye—Rita!"

"Goodbye—Cliff," she answered, the dimple showing at the corner of her mouth. "Or rather, *hasta luego,* as the Mexicans say."

"*Hasta luego* (till we meet again)," he repeated. His pulses quickened as he watched her cross the porch. At the door she turned to wave to him, and then vanished inside the house.

As he mounted his horse and rode away, Cliff Hardy felt that his call on Basset Shaw had turned out to be a ludicrous failure. He had been all set to tell Shaw off properly, and he had ended up having dinner with him and smoking his cigar!

"And *she's* to blame for it all," he complained querulously to Rojo. "How could I light into her uncle with her sitting right there? Women always tangle a man's twine for him, one way or another; but, horse, she's as pretty as a spotted pony hitched to a little red wagon! And the granddaughter of Sostenes l'Archevêque! What *am* I letting myself in for!"

The shadows were already long, and Hardy had no hankering for a night ride back to Amarillo, even had his horse been in condition for the trip, which he wasn't. Krause and Robinson's livery stable near the corner of Water and Main provided suitable accommodations for Rojo, and Hardy got a room for the night at the Exchange Hotel nearby.

For some time he sat by the open window smoking and thinking, while the lovely blue dusk sifted down like palpable dust and lights began winking through the gloom. Tascosa's mutter was rising to a rumble that by midnight would be a low roar, for business picked up in the Cowboy Capital during the hours of darkness.

After a while, Hardy pinched out his cigarrette and descended the stairs to the street. He had been in Tascosa a number of times before, was familiar with the lay of the town and had always found it interesting. He sauntered along Main Street toward McMasters, pushing his way through a jostling and turbulent crowd. Curiosity drew him to Basset Shaw's place.

When Hardy entered the big saloon, Basset Shaw was standing at the far end of the bar, smoking a cigar. He nodded but did not speak. Hardy ordered a drink and gave the place the once-over.

The building was of adobe construction and had two large rooms about eighteen feet wide by more than twenty feet long. A huge cottonwood beam in the center of the main room helped support the roof. A round column made of finished lumber had been built around the stout cottonwood post and doubtless provided welcome shelter for disinterested patrons when bullets were flying, as had been the case more than once. The bar extended across the east side of the main room. In the northwest corner was a small raised platform on which always stood five or six barrels of whiskey. It was said that once during a ruckus a bullet had pierced one of the barrels, but a cowboy with great presence of mind had thrust his finger into the hole and kept it there till order was restored, thereby preventing a lamentable waste of good liquor.

The second or back room was reached through an open archway and was used largely for gambling purposes. Dance-hall girls were permitted in this room but not in the main room or at the bar. Apparently Shaw had puritanical views concerning such matters.

Glancing again toward the end of the bar, Hardy did not see Shaw. Doubtless he had entered the back room or perhaps the little cubbyhole off it which served as an office. Anyhow, he was nowhere in sight.

Hardy had a couple of drinks and left. A little later he entered the famous Equity Bar, which faced south on Main Street and was Tascosa's largest and best known saloon. It had been established by Jack Ryan, former XT range boss, and had passed to various owners, including Jim East, Oldham County sheriff, who had killed Tom Clark the gambler in a gun battle in the Equity, and Button Griffin.

Business was also booming in the Equity. Hardy had a couple more drinks and wandered out. Next he visited the Jenkins and Dunn saloon at the corner of Spring Street and had a couple more. He was beginning to experience a comfortable glow. The pall of depression that had settled on him earlier in the evening had lifted and he was taking a quickening interest in things.

He repaired to the Cattleman's Exchange Bar and downed a couple more slugs of red-eye. He was developing a feeling of restlessness and a desire for action of some kind. He considered a few hands of poker but was deterred by an aversion to sitting still in one place. He took to the streets.

Hardy had consumed considerable straight whiskey, but not enough to drown reason altogether. He knew, circumstances being what they were, that he had no business roaming around the more questionable portions of Tascosa, such as East Tascosa, or Hogtown, as it was popularly dubbed, or the even more dubious terrain of the Rinehart Addition that centered around Bridge and Second Streets on the river front. But his restlessness was growing, and that dangerous craving for action. He wandered east to Hogtown and had a drink in the Edwards Hotel bar, and another in Captain Jinks' saloon and dance hall. Things appeared rather quieter than usual in Hogtown, and Hardy soon tired of his environment. He turned west again and walked to Bridge Street. At the corner he paused, then turned south. Down there was the "lower town," whose reputation was even more dubious than Hogtown's, a poorly lighted section with here and there shadowy little saloons and gambling houses that crouched furtively under the dank mists rising from the river.

Hardy was still very much on the alert. He took in his surroundings and frequently slanted a quick glance over his shoulder. He had covered perhaps a hundred paces when one of his backward glances caught four men just rounding the corner. They walked purposefully as if they knew exactly where they were going and why, but there was a feline stealthiness to their step that hinted at a desire to remain as inconspicuous as possible.

Hardy did some fast thinking. Of course the quartette might be going about some legitimate business of their own and have no interest in him; but then again they might not. He'd try to find out; he was still in a well lighted portion of the street. He slowed down a little; a quick glance showed him that the men behind had also slowed down. And when a moment later he quickened his step, they also speeded up. Hardy suddenly realized that he was on considerable of a spot; the four were undoubtedly stalking him, and for no good purpose. The question was, what to do? He had no desire to shoot it out with them—the odds against him were a bit heavy. It looked as if the only thing were to keep walking. He had a pretty good opinion of his own fleetness of foot and felt that if it came to a race he'd have a fairly good chance of outdistancing his pursuers. He walked on unconcernedly as the light grew dimmer. Not far ahead was a glow that seeped through the dusty windows of a little saloon almost at the water's edge. All around the building the gloom was intense. And only a few yards beyond was the bridge across the Canadian.

And then abruptly Hardy saw something that gave him no little concern. A vagrant beam of light showed three almost formless figures by the bridge head. It began to look very much as though he were trapped.

He evaluated the situation swiftly. If he tried to dash across the street, he would provide an excellent target; and there would be no turning aside because of a high, strong wire fence that shut off the neighboring lumberyard from the sidewalk. The saloon with the lighted windows? Very likely the bunch had taken that into consideration and perhaps hoped he would turn in there. Then in all probability he *would* be trapped. He was less than fifty paces from the building now, drawing uncomfortably close to the men by the bridge head.

And then he saw something else, something encouraging. Just before he reached the building he would be in black shadow. The rear of the building rested on stout piling, and encroaching on it was a low retaining wall which protected the sidewalk from being undermined and sliding down the slope. Under the building he would have a fighting chance, at least. He quickened his step and, when he reached the patch of shadow, dashed forward at top speed. He swung over the low stone wall and wormed and slid around until he was crouched in utter darkness beside one of the piles. Another moment and he heard the swift steps of the men approaching from the north, then a low mutter of words.

"Where the blazes did he go?" a voice exclaimed. "Hey, over there, where'd he go?"

Steps pattered up from the south. There was more low-voiced talk. Evidently the killers had not yet thought of the hideout under the building.

"Watch that bridge," a voice exclaimed. "He must have got past here somehow and may try to cross it. You fellows had better get back there."

Hardy had an inspiration. He groped frantically about till his hand encountered a smooth boulder somewhat larger than his fist. He edged forward a little, took good aim and tossed it underhand toward the bridge head only a few yards distant. It hit the floor boards and went bumping along, giving a creditable imitation of boots pounding the boards.

"There he goes!" shouted a voice. "After him! After him!"

Boots pounded away toward the bridge head;

there was a stutter of shots as the "pursuers" threw lead at the figure they couldn't see but which they felt must be hemmed in by the bridge rails.

In the saloon over Hardy's head sounded a muffled babble of voices, then silence. It looked as if nobody were coming out to see what was going on; doubtless an unhealthy practice in this locality. Hardy waited a few minutes longer, then stole his way back up the slope to the retaining wall. He levered himself over it, surged erect, and came face to face with a man who had just turned the corner of the building.

The fellow instantly went for his gun, but Hardy was faster. He caught the other's wrist and whirled him around. At the same moment his other hand clamped over the man's mouth and chin, stifling his yell to a gurgle. The man fought furiously, lashing out with his free hand, but Hardy kept behind him, his relentless grip forcing the man's head back till his chin was pointing skyward. Then with every atom of his strength, he wrenched sideways.

There was a soft snapping sound, as if a wet stick had been broken. The man's body jerked and flopped, his heels beating a queer, spasmodic tattoo on the ground. He shuddered from head to foot and went limp. Hardy let go of the flaccid wrist, gripped the body by the cartridge belt encircling its waist and hurled it over the retaining wall; it struck the ground with a sodden thump. Hardy headed up the street at a fast pace. Behind him sounded shouts, drawing nearer, but he was swiftly approaching the busy, well lighted section of the town and paid them no mind. Five minutes later he entered Basset Shaw's saloon.

Shaw was at the far end of the bar, evidently his customary place, smoking a cigar as usual. Hardy walked to within arm's length of him.

"Think I'll have that drink on the house," he said.

The purplish gleam was in Shaw's eyes, but he merely nodded and motioned to a bartender. Hardy raised the brimming glass to his lips and smiled thinly.

"Shaw," he said, "the tally's going up. *Here's to number six!*"

He downed the drink at a swallow, placed the empty glass on the bar, and smiled again, a thin, wolfish smile that showed his clenched teeth. Then he turned his back on Shaw and left the saloon.

Basset Shaw watched him go; on his usually expressionless face was a look of baffled bewilderment, tinged with the gray shadow of fear.

CHAPTER XI

Cliff Hardy decided he had had enough excitement for one night and went to bed. Early morning found him on his way back to Amarillo. He rode warily, although he had little fear of being molested on the open and well travelled trail. Also, he felt that Shaw's henchmen might well be developing a certain hesitancy over undertaking the chore of killing him. So far the results, from their point of view, had not been satisfactory.

Not that he believed for an instant that Shaw would give up so easily. As he had said, he usually got what he went after, doubtless largely through dogged persistence. And Shaw could hire plenty of men who would tackle anything if the price was high enough. Hardy knew very well that until Basset Shaw was taken care of, he walked in the shadow of death's wing. And so far he had nothing on Shaw that would justify his killing the old hellion.

Besides, now he didn't want to have to kill Basset Shaw. There was a reason—a reason that had to do with big blue eyes, dark curly hair, and a trim figure. He swore an exasperated oath.

Rojo craned his neck to look back at his master, and it seemed to Hardy that in his liquid brown eyes was a derisive glint. He swore again, amiably, and tickled the sorrel's ribs with his spurs. Rojo snorted immediately put on an exhibition of weaving, sunfishing and cloud-hunting that would have quickly pitched a less finished rider on his ear. Hardy chuckled, and straightened him out.

"You've tried that before, jughead, and you know it won't work," he said. "Jog along! We've got places to go and things to do."

Hardy did have plenty to do, but before riding to his ranch the following morning he stopped for a chat with Sheriff Nance.

"Well," said the sheriff, "I was over to the courthouse taking a look at the land transfers that just came in, and I see you have a new neighbor."

Hardy received the news with interest.

"Who is it?" he asked.

"Your friend Basset Shaw. He bought land

on both sides of your holding; bought plenty."

"The devil he did!" Hardy exclaimed. "I saw him day before yesterday and he didn't say anything about it."

"He never says anything about anything he doesn't have to," replied the sheriff. "How come you saw him?"

"He bought my note the bank held, and I rode to Tascosa to pay it off," Hardy explained.

"Fireworks?"

"Nope," Hardy answered. "I had dinner with him, and he gave me a cigar—and a drink on the house."

Sheriff Nance shook his head. "Sometimes I don't know which is harder to understand, Basset Shaw or you," he complained.

"His niece lives with him," Hardy remarked with elaborate casualness.

"Uh-huh, Rita Sostenes," said the sheriff. "I knew her dad well, a fine feller. Not much like *his* dad, who was a hell raiser for fair. Took five men to kill him, and he left his mark on all of them."

"She seems to be a nice girl," Hardy observed hesitantly.

The sheriff's eyes crinkled a little at the corners. "Why shouldn't she be?" he asked.

"Well—" Hardy began.

"Because she is Sostenes l'Archevêque's granddaughter and Basset Shaw's niece?" interrupted the sheriff. "Doesn't mean a thing. And, son, don't go climbing up your own family tree too high; you might find something hanging there."

"Wouldn't be a bit surprised," Hardy admitted with a grin. "But what do you suppose is Shaw's reason for buying that land? What has he got in mind?"

"Hard to tell," replied the sheriff. "What you want to keep in mind is that you control the water it takes to make most of that land really worth while."

"I will," Hardy promised. "I have reason to."

The sheriff nodded. "Maybe I've been sticking my nose in where I have no business to," he resumed, "but I've sort of developed an interest in this ruckus. I did a little snooping and learned that Shaw tried to buy up the land south of your holdings, but it 'pears you got the jump on him. He moved a mite too slow, because of which I expect he's kicking himself right now. If he'd gotten title to that strip, he'd have you where the hair is short."

"That's what I figured when I borrowed the money to get title to the strip," Hardy said. "He could have fenced me in, all right, and big outfits have done that to small owners and gotten away with it."

Hardy was right. It was a rather malodorous chapter in the saga of cattleland. Some of the big companies bought land completely surrounding the holdings of nesters and small owners and refused to give them ingress or exit. The little fellows were forced to sell at the prices offered, which all too often were disgracefully low.

"And it would have been up to me either to shoot my way out or face a long court battle which I would very likely have lost," Hardy observed to the sheriff. "I haven't got a barrel of money to hire smart lawyers and spend where it would do the most good, like Shaw has. Guess I was lucky to get the jump on him."

"Lucky, or smart," said the sheriff. "Little of both, I reckon. If Shaw had thought of that method first off he'd have done a better job. Maybe he did think of it, but I've a notion he doesn't like to spend money if he doesn't have to and decided to try cheaper methods first, like knocking out your wagon train, or killing you. Doesn't cost much to have a man killed in this section."

"Maybe not in money," Hardy conceded, "but sometimes the price in time is a bit high."

"Time?"

"That's right," Hardy replied. "Sometimes the gents who take over the chore all of a sudden don't have enough of it left to buy a drink, unless they sell whiskey in the hereafter, which I doubt."

"You may have a point there," the sheriff admitted. "How many did you kill in Tascosa?"

"One," Hardy answered, and left the office.

Hardy had intended riding to his ranch without delay, but he abruptly changed his mind. He entered the Ace-Full saloon, bought a drink and proceeded to do some hard thinking.

Hardy checked over the money he had on hand, and estimated what he could expect from his bone picking business during the next couple of months, being careful not to be too optimistic. Then he arrived at a decision, a decision that he well knew would not endear him to the old-time cowmen of the section. But there was no use trying to put back the clock, to stay the wheels of progress. And he had no intention of going down to ruin in defense of an outmoded tradition. A stern fact must be recognized—the day of the open range was ended. Those who refused to accept this would soon become as extinct as would the open range itself. Hardy was determined not to become extinct in this particular fashion. He borrowed some paper and a pencil from the bartender and covered the sheets with figures. Then he went to the railroad office and dispatched an order to the Glidden Company in Fort Worth, manufacturers of barbed wire.

When he arrived at the Four Sixes, Hardy found everything going smoothly. The ranchhouse, a comfortable dwelling, was nearly finished, as was the commodious new bunkhouse.

"Another week and we'll be all set," said Tom Cameron. "Everything taken care of in town?"

"Everything," Hardy replied.

"What's next in line?" Cameron asked.

"You'll be surprised," Hardy replied, with a grin.

Cameron was surprised and a bit shocked, and so were the Four Sixes cowboys, when freighting wagons delivered the spools of barbed wire to the ranch. But all had learned that arguing with their quiet boss was an unhealthy business, and there was little comment.

Due to the slowdown in bone picking, there were plenty of unemployed in and around Amarillo. Hardy had no difficulty hiring post hole diggers and wire stringers to assist his hands. Posts were a more serious problem, for there was little timber to be had in the plains country aside from the thickets and growth along the Canadian.

Hardy, however, had a talk with Colonel Goodnight. As a result, posts were cut in the Palo Duro and snaked out of the canyon by means of strong wire pulleys and then hauled to the ranch on heavy wagons.

The common practice in fence building was to use four strands of wire with three wire stays between posts about forty feet apart. Hardy, however, used four strands and spaced his posts twenty-five feet apart.

"Takes a little more time and work and costs a little more, but when we're through we'll have a fence that can't be knocked down easily," he told Cameron, adding, "and a fence the average horse can't jump, which may come in handy sometime."

"You're right about that," agreed the range boss. "Any gent who wants to get onto our range for some reason or other, likely a bad one, will have to cut the wire, which may slow him up at a time when he ain't got none to spare."

Where the Amarillo-Fort Worth Trail crossed his holdings, Hardy turned the fence, so that the barbed strands paralleled the broad trail on either side. This gave him two pastures, the south pasture being much the smaller of the two, which made working the cattle easier.

"But we'll only use the south pasture in summer," he told Cameron. "If a bad blizzard comes down from the north, the critters won't face it. They'll drift south till the fence stops them; then they'll bunch against it and freeze. So long as cows can move in a blizzard they'll make out, but not standing still. So after the fall roundup and after the beef herd is cut out for shipping, we'll drive everything onto the north pasture. Then if a bad storm appears to be on the way, we'll herd them north into the canyons and brakes. Once there, they'll stay sheltered till the storm blows itself out. I'll bet we don't lose a dozen head because of snow this winter."

There was no need to fence the north boundary of the ranch. There, the broken ground bordering the Canadian provided an effectual barrier and prevented straying on the part of the Four Sixes cows or trespassing by animals from other outfits.

In less then thirty days the chore was done. Hardy surveyed the result with satisfaction.

"I'm just about broken again," he confided to Cameron, "but it'll pay off in the end. We won't have to go rounding up the mavericking devils all over the Panhandle, and we'll be a lot better protected against stealing. Now if something unexpected doesn't bust loose, we should find it easy riding for a while."

"But it's just what you don't expect that usually does bust loose in cow country," the range boss replied prophetically.

Now that his fence was taken care of, Hardy decided to risk entering the lion's den again. So he blithely rode to Tascosa, stabled his horse and walked to Basset Shaw's residence on Spring Street.

This time there was no slender, graceful figure in blue sitting on the veranda, but when he knocked she opened the door.

"Well, I'll be darned!" she exclaimed. "So you *did* come back!"

"I told you I would," he replied.

"Oh, of course you did," she said, "but a man always says that, and usually doesn't mean it, or forgets all about it. Come in. Did you want to see Uncle Basset on business again?"

"Nope," he replied as he entered and closed the door.

"Because you won't," she explained. "He's in Dodge City."

Hardy thought this bit of news very encouraging.

She led him into a comfortably furnished living room. "Sit down," she said, "while I go tell the cook to set another plate; it's nearly dinner time."

They had a very pleasant dinner together, and

afterward they sat and talked in the living room for a while. Gradually both fell silent. Hardy smoked, while Rita regarded him through the silken fringe of her black and astonishingly long lashes.

Cliff Hardy was given to making quick decisions, and he believed in direct methods.

"Rita," he said, "will you marry me?"

The dimple at the corner of her mouth showed. She was silent for another moment. Then:

"I suppose I should give you the conventional answer and say, 'This is so sudden!' but I won't."

"Won't marry me?"

"Won't say, 'This is so sudden!' "

"Then you will?"

"Didn't I just say I won't?"

"Won't what?"

"Won't say, 'This is so sudden!' "

"Hang it all!" he exclaimed in exasperation. "You know what I mean!"

She laughed outright, and Hardy thought the sound was like little tinkling silver bells.

"Of course I do, and of course I will," she replied. "I made up my mind to that the first time I laid eyes on you; that is, if you asked me, as I had a notion you would, sooner or later. Do you think a girl would throw over the chance of getting a successful bone picker for a husband?"

"Bone picker!" he sputtered. "So this is what's called love and romance! Sounds more like a discussion in a slaughterhouse!"

She laughed again, very merrily. "Cliff, dear," she said, "I've a notion that real love and real romance are usually just like this. When two people can laugh at and with one another, and be natural, and not have to go hunting flowery phrases to express what they mean, what more do you want?"

"I'll show you," he said. And he did.

"Heavenly days!" she gasped, several minutes later. "Bone picker! Bone breaker is more like it! I don't believe I've got a whole rib left in my body! But I don't mind. Go ahead and break some more!"

For quite a while they were thoroughly occupied with each other, to the exclusion of all else. But the hard facts of life insisted on intruding themselves even in the Elysian Fields.

"Rita," Hardy said suddenly, "there's something I've got to tell you: your uncle and I don't get along."

Her reply surprised and startled him.

"I know that without your telling me," she said.

"How? Did *he* tell you?"

"No," she answered. "He never tells anybody anything he doesn't have to. When you were here the first time, I listened a little."

"Wasn't that rather unladylike?"

"Yes, but very feminine. I didn't hear everything that was said, but I gathered that he threatened you."

Hardy was silent.

She turned in his arms to face him. "Cliff," she said, "I wish you and Uncle Basset could get along together, and because I wish it, I'm going to ask you something, something it's very hard to ask. I want to marry you, my darling, right away. But I'm going to ask you to wait a while, in the hope that things will change."

The big blue eyes were misty now, and her red lips trembled. Hardy was silent for a moment; then he said heavily:

"I'll wait."

She did not speak, but her kiss was ample reward. Then she drew back and looked at him fondly, her eyes shining.

"I asked you because I hate to leave him now," she said. "He is so lonely and embittered. At times I really think he is a little insane. It seems to me his eyes show it at times. But he has been the soul of kindness to me, and it would be mighty poor appreciation for all he has done for me to walk out on him abruptly. I think that after a while I can make him understand and perhaps bring you two together. That is what I hope, and that is why I'm asking for a little time to try and see what I can do. I'll tell you his story as my mother told it to me; perhaps it will help you understand why he does the things they say he does."

"I'd like to hear it," Hardy replied.

"His father was a small rancher," she resumed. "The big owners hemmed him in and eventually caused him to lose his ranch. Later he was killed—murdered, it was said, by hired gunmen brought in by the big owners. Uncle Basset was little more than a boy then, and his sister, my mother, was much younger. But he went to work and supported his mother and little sister. It wasn't easy. There were plenty of times when they didn't even have enough to eat. My grandmother died young, worn out by the struggle, but Basset Shaw cared for his sister and kept a sort of home together until she grew up. But he was filled with hatred—hatred for everybody except her. He grew up to believe firmly that might is right, that only the ruthless can survive. He survived, and grew rich and influential, but his hatred for his fellows, especially those who were successful, increased as the years passed by. I think he instinctively hates anyone who appears likely to become successful. An unreasoning hate, but very real. His sister, the only person he loved, met my father, a fine man despite the fact that *his* father, Sostenes l'Archevêque, was an outlaw and killer. I think that the only reason Uncle Basset consented to the marriage was that Sostenes l'Archevêque's father was also killed unjustly. It forged a bond of sympathy between them, as it were. When my mother, who was already a widow at the time, died, Uncle Basset wanted me to come and live with him, and although Father's people, the Sostenes, were dubious as to the wisdom of my decision, I did. Although he never appears to show it, I feel that he is very fond of me, all he has left in the world. And now do you understand why I asked you to wait a little, my dear?"

Hardy nodded. The story he had just listened to was an old story in cattleland: the small owner gradually frozen out by the arrogant barons of the open range. If he fought back too strongly—he was murdered!

Yes, Hardy understood Basset Shaw better now, and he thought Shaw fortunate in having such an advocate to present his case in the best possible light.

CHAPTER XII

When Cliff Hardy rode back to Amarillo the following morning, he was in a very perturbed frame of mind. His thoughts fluttered around like startled birds and, like the birds, refused to settle, perhaps for lack of anything concrete to perch on. Somehow, Basset Shaw must be outsmarted and brought to terms. But how? Hardy hadn't the slightest notion. But he did know that the situation as it now stood put him in an impossible position as far as Rita was concerned. He couldn't ask her abruptly to leave Shaw, and if he did and she consented, there would still remain the conflict between her uncle and him, a source of perpetual worry and apprehension for her.

At length, with a shrug of his broad shoulders, he dismissed the whole aggravating matter and let his thoughts dwell exclusively on Rita.

Which was a sensible thing for a young man in the ardor of first love to do.

Cattle were pouring into the Panhandle. They had been coming for some years, but now the dam had burst and the tide was really sweeping the Staked Plains. From the crowded pastures of the Brazos, the Trinity, the Nueces and other parts they came, a continuous and irresistible flood of thudding hoofs and clashing horns, equalling the vanished herds of buffalo that once were the sole denizens of *Llano Estacado*.

Most historians of cattleland are content to deal with such great outfits as the XIT, the JA and their contemporaries with their vast acreage and their tremendous herds, passing over the ever increasing number of "little" ranches that in the aggregate counted more head than the big fellows. These were dotting the prairie country with a multitude of strange brands; brands the big outfits were wont wrathfully to declare could be too easily manufactured from such illustrious burns as the XIT, the JA, the LT, and the Frying Pan.

Be that as it may, small spreads were appearing everywhere, and their herds grew apace. Rustling was rampant, and gun fights between the small owners and the hands of the big outfits were becoming more and more frequent. The custom of hiring professional gunmen to do the fighting was becoming uncomfortably prevalent.

Cliff Hardy watched these developments with interest. Bone picking was still profitable and his wagons still ranged far and wide. Hardy was able to buy five hundred more head of improved stock from Silas Releford and an equal number of the better grade of longhorns from Colonel Goodnight. His herd was assuming respectable proportions.

Rustling was on the increase, becoming more prevalent than it had ever been before, and there was a changed public attitude toward many of those who practiced it. Time was when the rustler had been looked down upon by his neighbors, whose attitude toward him was the same as toward any other thief. But no longer was the widelooper who mavericked a few calves from such giants as the XIT, for instance, ostracized. The small ranchers and citizens in general held no brief for the big fellows. The only reason *they* didn't go in for widelooping, the average small owner held, was because they had already "stolen" everything in sight.

Under prevailing conditions, it was inevitable that another deplorable development should occur. The owners began taking the law in their own hands, especially the larger outfits. They

hired professional gunslingers to battle the
rustlers. The rustlers and those in sympathy
with them fought back. The result was a number
of corpse-and-cartridge sessions with a high
mortality rate.

With his fairly small, compact ranch strategi-
cally located and fenced, and with his cattle
now concentrated on the north range against the
threat of winter, Cliff Hardy was not much concerned over rustling, although he kept a close
watch on his cows. There was little likelihood
that his slow, heavily fleshed improved stock
would be tampered with, but it was not beyond
the realm of possibility that a swift and daring
raid might cut out a herd of his longhorns and,
following little known trails through the rough
country of the Canadian Valley, run them across
the New Mexico line. It would be a long drive
and a hard one, but wideloopers had successfully
made such before. So Hardy took no chances.
He guarded against stealthy pilfering by way of
the canyons where his north range stretched to
the bank of the Canadian. Such stealing, if not
checked, could spell disaster for a rancher. Un-
branded calves, of which there were already
many, were especially vulnerable. Once spirited
away, they could be branded and identification
by the rightful owner made impossible.

All over the Panhandle new ranches were springing up, but on either side of Hardy's holdings were broad stretches of untenanted prairie. It appeared that Basset Shaw was doing nothing about his extensive acreage, doubtless because a good part of it, as cattle land, was dependent on the precious water Cliff Hardy had fenced in.

At times horsemen were seen riding slowly over the land, as if checking conditions; but they never came very close to Hardy's wire, although every now and then it was plain their gaze was cast in that direction.

"Wouldn't be a bit surprised if they're some of Shaw's hellions looking us over, and with no good in mind," declared the suspicious Bill Jasper.

"Nothing to see he doesn't already know," Tom Cameron pointed out. The other hands were inclined to agree with Cameron, but Jasper remained suspicious of the unknown riders' intentions.

CHAPTER XIII

Meanwhile, Cliff Hardy had things other than mysterious horsemen to concern him; among them, the weather. One evening clouds began banking up in the northwest, and by night-fall the whole vast sweep of the heavens was one leaden arch. There was a damp chill in the air and an unpleasant heaviness.

Shortly before midnight, Hardy went out for a look around. The moon and the stars were hidden, yet a faint and lurid light shone now in one quarter of the heavens, now in another. He developed the queer conviction that the sky was sinking down upon the earth. There was no wind, but the air moaned audibly. It was as though the end of the world were near; all nature seemed to be big with impending disaster.

Hardy returned to the ranchhouse in a dis-turbed frame of mind. That ominous, downward-pressing sky, the shuddering air and the bitter chill presaged trouble. He only hoped the coming storm would hold off till daylight.

It did. Daylight brought the same gray, clouded sky and the same damp cold. Hardy decided on action.

"We're going to round up every cow and run them north to the canyons," he told Cameron. "If there isn't a blizzard coming, and a bad one, I miss my guess. Once up there they'll be safe. Otherwise they'll drift against the south fence and freeze; they'll never face a bad storm to get to shelter."

"Cows are stupid that way," Cameron agreed. "From the fool things they do, sometimes I think they're almost human."

The cowboys went to work. The cattle were combed out and started north. Back and forth the hands rode, gathering together the scattered bunches and single animals. By mid-afternoon almost all of the Four Sixes cows were on the move. The task was simplified by the fact that the beeves were in the habit of frequenting the banks of the stream after eating their fill in the early morning hours.

"There never was a better range to work," declared Cameron. "Long and narrow, with the creek running down the middle."

"We're lucky it is," said Hardy, glancing at the lowering sky. "We'll be getting snow any minute now."

"Other folks seem to have the same notion," replied Cameron, glancing westward—they were near the west wire at the moment. "Way over there go a couple of jiggers who're heading for town in a hurry."

Hardy nodded. "I saw them half an hour ago," he said. "They were coming up from the south, not far from the wire; then they turned west." He gazed after the bouncing blobs that were the receding riders.

"They're sure sifting sand now," he added. "We'd better sift some too; there's the first snowflake."

A little later, the flakes really were beginning to fly. Hardy glanced over his shoulder.

"Now what the devil?" he wondered. "If that isn't our chuck wagon headed this way, I'm losing my eyesight."

"You ain't losing it," Cameron returned, gazing at the approaching vehicle. "That's the wagon, all right, and old Pete, the cook, is driving. Now what do you suppose has gotten into that loco hellion?"

They reined in and waited till the lumbering wagon drew near.

"What's the notion?" Hardy shouted. "You out for a ride?"

"I'm out to cook some dinner for you terrapin-brained centipedes," the irascible old cook bellowed in reply.

"Well, we were coming back for a late supper," Hardy told him. "Do you think it'll take us a week to run those critters to the canyons?"

"You ain't going to eat supper at the ranch-house, nor breakfast, either," Pete answered. "You're going to hole up under a cliff in a canyon tonight and be darned glad you found one. I've been through this sort of thing before and I know the signs. It's going to be a sock-dollager, and don't you forget it. There won't be any making it back to the *casa* this night. Shut up and don't argue with me! I was shoving cows through blizzards before you had any teeth. *I* know what I'm talking about."

Old Peter was right. The thickening flakes were the beginning of the worst blizzard the Panhandle had ever experienced.

Long before the northern canyons and gorges were reached, the snow was drifting down in clouds, swirling and eddying before an ever increasing wind from the north. And what had been a routine chore had become a terrific task. The cattle didn't want to face the howling blasts.

They continually tried to turn and drift with the storm. It took every possible effort the cursing cowboys could put forth to keep them slogging ahead. The prairie was a raving white waste, the cold growing more bitter by the minute. Old Pete, urging his straining horses to do their darnedest, cursed the storm, Texas, and the day he was born.

"Another mile and we'll be shoving them into shelter," Hardy bawled above the bellow of the wind. "We'll make it."

"But we ain't never going to be the same again," Bill Jasper roared reply. "I ain't never seen anything like this. My horse is covered with ice."

Jasper's remark recalled something to Hardy's mind. He turned Rojo and rode back till he was alongside the laboring wagon.

"Pete," he shouted, "there were horses in the corral when we left this morning; did you shove them into the barn before you pulled out?"

"No, by gosh, I didn't," the cook yelled in reply. "I forgot all about them. I was so busy getting the infernal wagon loaded I never paid them no mind."

"A slip anybody could make; don't worry about it," Hardy said. He turned Rojo and rode forward to where Cameron, a mounted wraith in the murk and gloom, was hammering the lag-

gards to the accompaniment of appalling profanity. Hardy leaned over and placed his lips
close to the range boss' ear.

"I'm heading back to the ranchhouse, Tom,"
he told him. "Got to get those horses out of the
exposed corral and into the stable. If they stay
there till this infernal thing blows itself out,
they'll be frozen stiff."

"You'll be taking a whale of a chance," Cameron protested. "It's almost night and the storm's
getting worse. Pete was right when he said we'd
have to hole up in a canyon. You're liable to
freeze, or get lost."

"No, I won't get lost," Hardy replied.

"Stick to the creek and you can't miss the
house," Cameron advised. "All you've got to do
is follow it and you'll get there okay."

Hardy didn't argue the point, but he had no
intention of following the windings of the stream
that would add miles to the distance to be trav-
ersed.

"Don't worry," he said. "Rojo will get me
through, all right. I'll be back up here as soon
as I can make it."

"Wait till the storm's over," Cameron said.
"We'll be okay up here. Everything's going
along fine; the lead cows are shoving into a
canyon right now."

Hardy nodded, turned Rojo and rode south.

At first he experienced a sense of relief at having the storm at his back; but the comfort garnered from his changed position didn't last long. The cold was becoming deadly, and the snow fell thicker and faster. Moreover, now it was more frozen sleet than snow. The wind howled like a thousand furies and swirled stinging particles into his face. He slapped his arms, beat his hands against his chest. Before he had gone five miles his legs, despite the warmth of the horse's body, were becoming wooden. Finally he dismounted and stumbled along on foot till the circulation started up again; but every couple of miles he was forced to repeat the exhausting performance.

He began to have qualms about his vaunted sense of direction; he had never before had to use it under such appalling conditions. Perhaps he *was* going wrong, veering too far to the west. If he was, there would be nothing to set him right till he butted up against the south wire. Then he would have to fight his way back in the face of the storm. He began to understand how panic overtook men lost in the snow and sent them to their death. He grimly shook the cobwebs from his mind and rode on, telling himself that he couldn't go wrong. He took some comfort from the thought that Rojo would surely head for the ranchhouse and the welcome shelter of his stall. But maybe horses got lost, too. He'd never given the contingency much thought. Now, all of a sudden, it was a disquieting possibility.

Rojo was slogging ahead steadily, as if he knew exactly where he was going, and he didn't seem perturbed or exhausted. Hardy knew the great sorrel's mighty strength and endurance and had little fear that he would falter. But *was* he going right!

He estimated the distance they must have covered. If he was figuring right, the ranchhouse must be less than two miles ahead. He strained his eyes to catch sight of the solid bulk of the building looming through the turmoil and the gloom. He didn't see it, but only a little while later he did see something, something for which he was unable to account. Somewhere above him and ahead of him, where the sky should have been, was a reddish glow.

What the devil could that be? he wondered. Was he growing delirious from pain and exhaustion? Seeing things? This was something else to worry about, as if he didn't have enough already. Abruptly he caught himself lurching sideways in the icy saddle. If he fell he was done for. He beat his chest, slapped his face vigorously with his open palm. The pain of the blow aroused him a little. He stared ahead, hoping he would not see the devilish glow. But he still saw it. It was no figment of his overwrought imagination. There could be but one explanation. Ahead something was burning.

Another moment and he saw what it was. He was in the ranchhouse yard before he realized it, and saw that the bunkhouse was burning fiercely.

How the devil did it catch? was his first instinctive thought. He had been certain that the fire in the stove had been extinguished before they'd ridden north. Evidently it hadn't been, and a coal had snapped out and fired the floor boards. He had pulled Rojo to a halt; now he started to urge him toward the burning building, then abruptly reined in again. There was a light in the ranchhouse kitchen, where no light had any business being.

The cold and the storm forgotten, he dismounted. Something was very much wrong and he had to find out what it was.

"Take it easy, feller," he whispered to Rojo. Bending his head against the beat of the wind, he circled the ranchhouse and reached the front porch. Careful to make no noise, although there was little chance of anything being heard above the bellow of the blizzard, he mounted the steps and crossed the porch to the front door, which was never locked. With the greatest care he turned the knob, waited till the storm let loose a loud roar, and opened the door. He slipped in, closing it behind him, and paused to listen. Coming from the rear of the house was a mumble of voices.

Hardy waited a moment, flexing his fingers vigorously to get the stiffness out of them. Then he crossed the living room with a noiseless tread. Beyond the living room was the dining room, and beyond that the kitchen. The far door of the dining room stood open, light from the kitchen pouring through it. Hardy slipped forward a few paces.

Now he could see into the kitchen. A lamp burned on the table, and by its light he saw four men busily heaping oil-soaked shavings and kindling wood against the far wall. He made sure his guns were not frozen in the sheaths, loosened them a little and took another step forward. He was almost to the open door when he trod on a loosely nailed board that gave under his foot and let loose a crack like a pistol shot.

The four men whirled at the sound. "Look out!" one yelled. An arm swept the lamp from the table. Through the darkness spurted reddish flame.

Hardy, who had hurled himself sideways, felt

the wind of passing lead. A slug burned a streak along his ribs. He jerked his guns and shot with both hands as fast as he could pull trigger. Answering shots streaked lances of light through the gloom. The building rocked to the roar of the reports.

Ducking, weaving, trying to keep out of a direct line with the open door, Hardy fired again and again. He heard a coughing grunt, then the thud of a falling body. A bullet twitched at his sleeve like a ghostly hand. From the kitchen came a wailing cry, then the clash and clatter of an overturned chair and a queer scratching and scraping as if fingernails were raking on wood.

And at the same instant, Cliff Hardy's head seemed to explode in one vast burst of fire and pain. He felt himself falling and clutched at the wall for support. Dimly through the welter of pain he heard the kitchen door bang open, letting in a blast of icy cold. Instinctively his fingers tightened on the triggers of his sagging guns. One boomed a last shot. The other clicked on an empty shell. Hardy was sliding down the wall, clawing vainly at the smooth surface. His guns clattered to the floor and he sank beside them in a motionless heap.

CHAPTER XIV

When Hardy finally regained consciousness he knew he must have been out for quite some time. He was numb with cold and his teeth were chattering. The icy blast still poured through the open kitchen door. His head was one tremendous ache and he was sick and giddy, but his mind was clearing. He got to a sitting position, holding his throbbing head in his hands till he gained sufficient strength to stagger erect, clutching the door jamb for support. Leaning against it, he fumbled a flat, tightly corked bottle from his pocket—the cowboy's waterproof matchbox. He managed to unstopper the bottle and extract a match which he struck on the door jamb. The wind instantly blew it out, but by the momentary flicker he saw that the path to the kitchen door was clear. He staggered to the door, kicked aside some of the drifted snow and closed it. Then he struck another match and lighted a bracket lamp beside the stove. The yellow flare showed two dead men lying on the floor, but for the moment Hardy paid them no attention. His first thought was for Rojo and the horses in the exposed corral; but he knew he must get some warmth into his numbed body before facing the outside.

He was grateful to the hellions who had tried to burn him out for one thing: they had left plenty of good fuel handy. He crammed the stove with shavings and kindling and struck a match to it. Almost at once he had a roaring blaze going, which he fed with more wood as fast as it burned down.

The stove heated quickly. He hovered over it, rubbing his hands and stamping his feet. His feeble pulses quickened and the blood began flowing normally through his body. An examination of his wounded head disclosed a slight furrow above his left temple at the hairline. The passing slug had done little more than break the skin, but it had hit him one whale of a wallop. The bleeding had already ceased, and the blood that had flowed from the wound was caked on his face.

With scarcely a glance at the two bodies, he retrieved his fallen hat from the dining room floor and jammed it on his head. Then he ejected the spent shells from his guns and replaced them with fresh cartridges. There was no cause to believe that the two firebugs who had escaped his bullets were still hanging around, but he was taking no chances. Finally, feeling up to the effort, he lighted a lantern and plowed out into the storm.

Rojo, who had evidently found makeshift shelter in the lee of the ranchhouse, came at his whistle and appeared little the worse for wear. With the sorrel plodding beside him, Hardy fought his way to the corral. The horses were bunched beside the gate, heads hanging, their coats sheathed with ice. After a struggle, Hardy got the gate open and called to them. They followed Rojo docilely, stepping stiffly, stumbling from time to time. Hardy led them to the barn and after another struggle managed to get the door open. He ran them inside and, after getting the rig off Rojo, rubbed them down as best he could. Then, after putting plenty of oats in the mangers, he staggered back to the house.

On the back of the stove was a half-filled pot of coffee bubbling away merrily. Hardy gratefully downed several steaming cups. Then he examined the bodies of the two men he had killed.

One was a lanky individual with a stubble of beard on his long blue chin. The other, short and stocky, was, Hardy decided, a Comanche breed, much the same type as the man he had killed in the bone canyon on the Canadian. He was too weak and sick to conduct a more thorough examination, but he did manage to drag the bodies into the front room and cover them with a blanket. He regarded them morosely.

"Eight!" he muttered. "I'm well on my way to passing Billy the Kid's record."

His strength was ebbing again and he experienced a queer numbness. He built up and banked the fire and then, fogged about with a blue haze of utter exhaustion, he tumbled into bed.

When Hardy awoke, greatly refreshed and, aside from a sore head, about his usual self again, the window panes were gray with wan light filtering through the swirling snow clouds. For the storm still raged with unabated fury. The house was icily cold, but he soon took care of that with a roaring fire in the kitchen stove. He was ravenously hungry and, after plowing through the drifts to the barn to make sure the horses' wants were cared for, set about throwing together a good breakfast. He ate hugely and drank numerous cups of coffee. Then, feeling placid and content, he rolled a cigarette and reviewed the night's happenings.

That he had suffered nothing worse than a destroyed bunkhouse and a skinned head, he felt was due to nothing but luck. Had Pete not forgotten to place the horses in the stable before pulling out with the chuck wagon, the firebugs would have had everything their way. House, barns and other buildings would have been destroyed, and that, with winter coming on apace, heralded by the frightful blizzard, would have been nothing less than a catastrophe.

Hardy finished his smoke and then gave the two bodies a more thorough examination. Their pockets revealed nothing of significance other than plenty of money in gold and silver. Hardy wondered if that money had been the price paid for the destruction of his buildings. If so, this pair hadn't gotten much enjoyment from it.

He decided to move the bodies to the porch. Now that the house was warm, they would get ripe a bit too quickly for comfort, and he didn't know how long he would have to stay holed up.

All that day the storm continued with unabated fury, and through the following night. When Hardy awoke on the second morning to see the white waste still swirling outside the windows, he began to worry a bit about his hands. Quite likely Pete had provisioned the wagon plentifully, but at this rate he'd need a grocery store and a butcher shop to keep going.

Then, just about noon, the snow ceased to fall. Overhead the clouds were sweeping southward before a strong wind, but at ground level there was complete calm. This continued for nearly an hour, until Hardy, busy shovelling paths through the drifts, felt a breath of warmer air fan his cheek. Another ten minutes, and the clouds curled up like the edges of torn paper and a funnel of brilliant sunlight poured through the opening. It broadened quickly at the base until the whole vast white of the prairie was bathed in a tremendous golden glow.

Hardy straightened and gazed around. There was nothing in sight; the broad sweep of the rangeland was utterly deserted. Overhead, the sky was purest blue, and from the south streamed the warm wind. In a matter of minutes the eaves were dripping. Hardy finished his paths, returned the horses to the corral so they could exercise a bit and walked over to glance at the irregular mound that had been the bunkhouse. Well, it wouldn't take long to build another, as soon as he could get the necessary lumber from Amarillo. He resolved to start work on the building without delay. He wasn't fooled by the misleading warmth pouring up from the south; the wind could change overnight and another blizzard come howling down from the northern reaches.

He went to the ranchhouse and cooked something to eat. The chances were good that the boys would be coming in by nightfall. He wondered how they had made out with the herd and felt rather sanguine. No reason the cows shouldn't have weathered the storm in the sheltered canyons where there was plenty of browse and they could paw away the snow and reach grass.

Just before dark the hands arrived, volleying questions as they stared at the snowy mound where the bunkhouse had formerly stood. After Hardy told them what had happened, the air was blue with profanity.

"Some day we're riding to Tascosa, and *Señor* Shaw will find himself the lead attraction of a necktie party," Tom Cameron declared. The others nodded grim assent.

"I've a notion those two riders we spotted as we were driving the cows north were keeping tab on us," Hardy said. "When they saw the chuck wagon roll, they figured we would all be gone for the night, and that gave them their chance."

"Nervy devils, taking a chance on that storm,"

commented Jasper.

"That sort will risk anything if the pay is high enough," growled Cameron. "Yes, that was it. As soon as they figured we'd be away all night, they rode to tell the others, who were waiting somewhere. Cold-blooded hellions! Well, a couple of the snakes got their come-uppance, anyhow. Pity you didn't bag all four, Cliff."

"If I hadn't decided I'd better take the wagon out, maybe it wouldn't have happened," observed old Pete.

"I think we all got a lucky break that you did," Hardy told him. "They would have known very well that you were alone here. Chances are you'd just have gotten yourself murdered in addition to everything going up in smoke. As it was, things worked out very well. How about the cows, Tom?"

"Fine and dandy," Cameron replied. "I don't believe we lost a calf. We shoved 'em into that big canyon west of the trail that leads to the bone canyon. Plenty of cover there and places where they can paw out grass. We holed up under a cliff overhang and made out okay. I'm afraid other outfits weren't so lucky. It was one whale of a storm, the worst I ever saw."

Later, when news from other spreads began filtering in, Cameron was proven a prophet. The loss of stock was appalling. Any number of the smaller outfits faced ruin, and even big companies felt the seriousness of the situation.

Nor was the Panhandle country alone affected by the disaster. The blizzard, which lasted much longer in the more northern states, killed several hundred thousand head of stock in Kansas and Colorado. Thirty to forty percent of Dakota and Montana cattle succumbed. In fact, it was estimated that fully one half of the cows in the northern country perished during that disastrous winter.

The Four Sixes bedded down in the ranchhouse for the night and were quite comfortable, there being plenty of room. Besides, old Pete had thoughtfully stowed the blankets from the bunkhouse in his chuck wagon before he set out after the herd prior to the storm, and the cowboys had often slept on worse beds than a warm ranchhouse floor.

Before midnight, the warm wind from the south brought rain which fell in torrents until mid-afternoon of the following day. As a result, the snow melted even faster than it had fallen, and another day found the prairie bare.

As soon as the rain let up a bit, Hardy and Cameron rode to Amarillo and contracted for the lumber and other materials necessary to the erection of a new bunkhouse. They also hired several handymen-carpenters who were glad to pick up an odd job in their slack season.

"We want to get it done as fast as possible," Hardy said. "Another infernal storm is liable to swoop down at any time. And," he added, "hereafter there'll always be a man staying at the house with Pete. We're not taking any chances, although I doubt Shaw will try it again. He's too original and resourceful to pull the same thing twice; he'll think up another beaut for his next attempt."

"I still think it would be a good notion to ride up there and hang him," Cameron growled.

Although, for personal reasons, Hardy couldn't subscribe to Tom's suggestions, he didn't argue the point; he was of the same mind himself.

After due deliberation, Hardy decided to tell Tom Cameron about Rita Sostenes. Cameron, a confirmed bachelor of forty, shook his head and whistled.

"Gentlemen, hush!" he remarked. "Now we're in for real trouble. Never fails when a female comes into the picture. Maybe it would have been better if Shaw had shot you long ago. Then you would have gotten it over with in a hurry, at least. What the blazes you going to do about it?"

"I don't know," Hardy admitted frankly, "but I do know I'm going to ride up to Tascosa tomorrow and have another talk with her."

"Okay, I'll ride with you," Cameron suggested.

Hardy refused the offer of company. "Don't want you," he replied. "I'll make out all right."

Cameron said nothing more, but when Hardy rode north the following morning, he was trailed by three grim figures—Tom Cameron, big Bill Jasper, and a taciturn, hard-bitten old cowboy named Walsh Baker, commonly known as "Slow" Baker. His nickname was a bit of gentle rangeland sarcasm in deference to the thirteen notches cut on the butt of his old Smith & Wesson single-action Forty-four. There were men who declared that Slow could dot a lizard's eye at twenty paces with that old Russian model hogleg, and dot the other eye before the lizard had time to tumble over.

"Cliff is a smart jigger, all right," Cameron told his companions, "but when even a smart man gets mixed up with a woman, he all of a sudden goes short of brains as a terrapin is of feathers. We'll just keep an eye on that addled hombre till he's back safe in the home corral."

When Hardy reached the Shaw residence, for the second time he received a pleasant surprise: Basset Shaw wasn't at home.

"He went to Cheyenne, the new town, this morning," Rita explained. "From there he's going to Amarillo; doesn't expect to be back for several days."

"What's he doing in Amarillo?" Hardy wondered.

"He said it was a business matter," Rita replied. "He didn't say any more."

Hardy had an uneasy premonition he might hear more about Shaw's "business matter" in due time. For the moment, however, he proceeded to make the most of his host's unexpected absence.

Much later, under the shadowy glow of the single small lamp, he asked:

"Honey, when are you going to marry me?"

"Perhaps I'm taking a chance by putting it off," Rita replied with a giggle. "I may end up losing you to another woman! But I am going to ask you to wait a little longer, say till after Christmas."

With this he had to be content.

It was well past midnight when Hardy kissed Rita goodnight and headed for his horse. He had decided to take the night ride back to Amarillo, Rojo having had plenty of rest.

The Krause and Robinson livery stable had been full when he'd arrived in Tascosa, and

Hardy had found accommodations for his horse at a little stable kept by a Mexican in the Rinehart's Addition. The most direct route was west on Mabry Avenue to Church Street, then south to Main and west to Bridge Street, the stable being situated in an alley between Grace and Bridge Streets and just south of First Street.

The route was a rather lonely one, the side streets being practically deserted, and Hardy was instinctively watchful, although with Shaw out of town he anticipated no trouble.

What Hardy failed to take into account was that Shaw's men were *not* out of town and were imbued with a desire to even the score with the man who had killed eight of their number.

Hardy reached First Street without incident, but as he neared the alley, a short distance to the west, he saw four men walking swiftly along First Street from the direction of Grace Street. He eyed them keenly and turned down the alley, quickening his step. He was almost to the stable door when he saw something that gave him considerable concern: there were men at the corner where the alley emptied onto First Street, fully a half-dozen of them. They started up the alley as at a prearranged signal.

Cliff Hardy did some swift, hard thinking. It began to look very much as if he were trapped.

Well, there was only one dubious sanctuary—
inside the adobe stable. The walls, while of soft,
sun-dried brick, were thick and would stop bullets; and perhaps he could hold the flimsy door,
if the bunch really meant business. He jerked
open the door and slipped inside. From the tail
of his eye he saw the men down the alley break
into a run. He pulled the door shut, and went
for his guns as a voice spoke from the dark in-
terior.

CHAPTER XV

"Hold it, Cliff!" said the voice. "It's me—Tom Cameron. Slow Baker and Bill Jasper are with me. What's going on outside? Are the sidewinders closing in on you?"

"Looks that way," Hardy answered quickly. "Coming from both ends of the alley—nearly a dozen of them. How did you fellows get here? Not that I'm not darned glad to see you."

"We trailed you to town," Cameron answered. "Been keeping an eye on you all night. Slow heard some talk in Shaw's rum hole and figured what was in the wind, so we slid in here to wait for you." His voice dropped to a whisper.

"Listen! Don't I hear somebody moving outside?"

"Yes," Hardy whispered back. "Get set!"

Tensely the cowboys waited. There was a scraping sound of boots outside the door, then a pattering rush. The door was flung violently open. Four men loomed against the starlight.

They were met by a hail of bullets as the Four Sixes bunch cut loose. One flopped grotesquely to the ground and lay still; a second went down kicking and clawing and rolling over and over away from the door. The other two dodged sideways out of range. The door swung shut of its own accord.

And thus began the big fight that would keep Tascosa talking for many a long day.

"The gunslingers didn't figure to run into four of us instead of one," Cameron chortled. "This ain't so bad."

"Liable not to be so good, though, when they get up the nerve to rush the door," Hardy answered. "They've still got us outnumbered. Keep down! They're shooting through that little window. Hope they won't plug the horses."

"They won't," said Cameron. "The horses are tied under a tree down at the corner of Bridge and Second Streets. Figured they'd be safer there, and handier; they're all rigged to go."

"Good notion," said Hardy. "Keep down!"

Bullets were whistling through the open window and plunking into the rear wall. Others slashed through the door. Then from the rear drifted the cool voice of old Slow Baker.

"You fellers hold the front for a while," said Slow. "I've found a shovel, and I'm digging a hole through the wall of this blasted mud shack. Give me ten minutes, and we'll slide out and hand those gents a surprise."

"Go to it!" Hardy whispered back. "We'll hold 'em."

Outside, the guns continued to bang. The air was full of the whine of lead and the solid thump of slugs burying themselves in the soft adobe. Between the crackle of the reports could be heard the rasp and scrape of old Slow's shovel.

A line of light showed between the door and the jamb. It widened. Something dark showed in the narrow opening. Hardy fired two quick shots, and the shadow vanished with a choking cry.

"You got him!" exulted Jasper. "Look out! Here they come!"

The door was banged open. Men jammed the opening, shooting and yelling. But the reception they got was too hot for them. They gave way before the storm of bullets. Hardy was pretty sure that a hit, maybe two, had been scored. Again slugs whined through the window. Slow Baker's shovel scraped steadily.

Then the shooting died down. Straining his ears, Hardy could hear a low mutter of voices.

"They're up to something," he told Cameron.

Tensely they waited, while old Slow's shovel scraped and scraped. There sounded a soft thud against the door, another and another.

"What the blazes?" wondered Jasper.

Another moment and he found out. The hue of the window abruptly changed from dusty silver to a gold-flecked ruddiness. There was a crackling and snapping. A pungent odor filled the air.

"They've fired the door!" exclaimed Hardy. "Figure to burn us out. And they'll do it, too, if we don't get a break. The roof's thatch, and dry. How you coming, Slow?"

"Couple more minutes," came a muffled reply. The shovel scraped faster.

"Where's the Mexican who owns this joint?" Hardy asked.

"At a saloon over in Hogtown, getting drunk on the pocketful of pesos we gave him to make himself scarce," Jasper replied. "Didn't see any sense in letting him stay here and maybe get plugged."

"We'll have to send him some more to pay for his shack," Hardy said. "Say, it's getting awful smoky in here."

It was, and very hot, too. Bullets were again whistling through the window, to discourage any attempt to escape by that route. Overhead, there was a tiny flicker that quickly widened to a tindery glow; the thatched roof had caught. A few more minutes and their position would be untenable. Slow's shovel had stopped scraping.

And then came the old cowboy's voice. "Okay," he said. "I got a hole big enough to crawl through. Come on, you jiggers."

Hurrying to the rear, they wormed their way through the ragged opening. It was a tight squeeze for Hardy and Jasper, but they finally made it at the expense of some skin. Outside, by the glare of the burning roof, they took stock of their surroundings.

They were hemmed in on all sides by the walls of 'dobes built back of the stable; it was evidently a Mexican quarter. At the northwest corner of the stable was a narrow opening that apparently led to the alley.

"This won't do," Hardy said. "If they catch us back here we're sitting quail. We've got to make it to the alley, rush them and head for the horses. All set? Let's go."

They hurried to the opening, cautiously entered it, and reached the alley without being detected. Grouped in front of the flaming building was a knot of men, all gazing toward the door that was almost burned away. The cowboys burst from the opening, yelling and shooting.

With howls of alarm the others scattered, firing back as fast as they could pull trigger, dashing for cover between the scattered buildings that lined the far side of the alley. Instantly the narrow expanse was a blazing inferno of bullets, smoke and blood.

Tom Cameron cursed viciously. "Got me in the arm!" he gulped. "Not bad!"

Another instant and Jasper reeled sideways, shifting his gun from his right to his left hand.

"Top of the shoulder!" he panted.

"Let's go!" roared Hardy, shooting with both hands. They raced down the alley into the deeper shadows, lead whining all around them, kicking up dust at their feet. Hardy assisted Jasper, who was staggering a little. Old Slow covered the rear, running backwards part of the time and firing methodically at the flashes from the openings between the buildings. Another moment and they ran from the alley and turned east on Second Street. They reached Bridge Street, and didn't take time to answer the questions shouted by scattered groups of citizens attracted by the uproar.

"To the right—under the tree," panted Cameron. "They're slip-tied. Jerk 'em loose and sift sand!"

Another moment and all were mounted and clattering across the bridge.

Two miles south of the Canadian, Hardy called a halt. "Want to look you fellows over," he told Cameron and Jasper.

"I'm okay," said the range boss. "I've tied a handkerchief around the arm and the bleedin's almost stopped; bone isn't busted. Oh, it don't hurt bad. I've cut myself worse shaving."

Jasper's wound was a bit more serious, a ragged furrow through the top of his left shoulder that had numbed his arm and was still bleeding. Hardy padded and bandaged it with neckerchiefs and fashioned a sling. He rolled a cigarette and placed it between Jasper's lips. After a few deep drags the big fellow declared he was all hunky-dory. They rode on at a swift pace, although they had little fear of pursuit.

"I've a notion they got a bellyful, all right," Hardy said. "We did for four or five, maybe more, and the chances are some more got nicked."

When they neared Amarillo, Hardy decided it would be best to circle the town and ride straight to the ranch.

"There'll be lots of excitement up there over what happened," he explained to his companions. "Best if nobody knows for sure we were mixed up in it."

The others agreed, and they did not draw rein till they reached the Four Sixes ranchhouse.

CHAPTER XVI

The town of Tascosa was dying. Barbed wire, and the decision of the Chicago, Rock Island and Gulf Railroad to build its line from Liberal, Kansas across the plains of Texas and into New Mexico some twenty miles north of the Canadian River, thus missing Tascosa by more than fifty miles, spelled doom for the Cowboy Capital. The new town of Delhart would become the division point and shop center Tascosa had hoped to be.

Barbed wire had turned aside the trail herds that were Tascosa's life blood. These herds were assembled from as far west as Phoenix, Arizona; Silver City, New Mexico; the Pecos country; and the Davis Mountain region of Texas. The loss of the trail herd business was fatal. The great ranches such as the XIT, the LIT, and the

LS had completely fenced their land and allowed no passage. The courts had upheld the right of ranch owners to fence their property, and stringent laws against wire cutting had been passed. Tascosa was slowly being "fenced in."

Items appeared in *The Pioneer* such as:

"J. M. Robinson and Bud Turner are erecting and operating a saloon in Grenada in Deaf Smith County."

and—

"Dave Adkinson, Bill Wheeler, George Knighton and Britt Roberts have moved to Hartley."

Then, about the middle of November, Cliff Hardy, who perused such items with interest, read:

"Another prominent Tascosan, Mr. Basset Shaw, has sold his business and will move to Amarillo, where he will set up a saloon and dance hall similar to his Tascosa establishment."

Without speaking, Hardy passed the paper to Bill Cameron.

"So the old hellion is moving in among us, eh?" remarked Cameron, after he had spelled out the item. "Well, anyhow, it'll keep you from going to Tascosa and risk getting shot up."

Hardy nodded grimly. He felt that the showdown with Basset Shaw was drawing near.

"Why the devil did he do it?" Cameron wondered.

"Because Tascosa's a dead duck and Amarillo's up and coming," Hardy replied. "Shaw is a smart business man and knows it, so he's trailing his twine."

"Folks say that Tascosa will boom when the Rock Island goes through there," Cameron remarked.

"The Rock Island's not going through there," Hardy stated flatly. "They'll bypass the rough Canadian River country and build across the level prairie to the north. I figure they'll cross the Canadian at Logan and build to Tucumcari, New Mexico, where their tracks will join with those of the Southern Pacific. They'll intersect the Forth Worth and Denver down in the southwest corner of Dallas County. Understand they're already laying out a town there to take care of the shops they're going to build. That'll be a division point. Tascosa will never see a railroad. The new town will grow fast, but Amarillo will pull away from it after a while. Amarillo is the coming town of the Panhandle, and gents with plenty of savvy, like Basset Shaw, figure to get in on the ground floor.

"And cut the ground out from under everybody else, if they can," he added, his voice hardening.

"Then I reckon it'll be up to us to do a little cutting of our own," Cameron said cheerfully. *"Señor* Shaw is liable to end up holding the hot end of the branding iron, and wishing he could let go. But what about the girl, Cliff?"

"That's what's got me bothered," grumbled Hardy. "She seems to sort of like the old hellion."

"Women and trouble just naturally go hand in hand," snorted Cameron. "Never knew it to fail."

Panhandle land values were steadily rising. For his first purchase, Cliff Hardy had paid but twenty cents an acre. The last strip he had bought had cost him five times more, and now the asking price of much less ideally located holdings was quadruple the latter figure.

Similar conditions prevailed all over the Staked Plains. A block of 265 square miles acquired by Colonel Goodnight only a few years before for twenty cents an acre was now quoted at ten times the original outlay, and the Colonel wasn't selling.

Neither was Cliff Hardy, although he could have disposed of his holdings at a handsome profit.

With his ample water supply and his sheltered north pasture, Hardy's land was rated considerably above the average in value, as was his stock. The cross of Herefords and longhorns was proving highly satisfactory. Hardy's ambition to own a cow factory that would pay appeared well on the way to realization.

"Yes, son, you sure showed yourself to be a smart hombre," observed Sheriff Nance one day not so long after the big fight in Tascosa, as Hardy sat in his office discussing various rangeland matters. "You've sure been getting the last laugh on folks. They laughed when you started bone picking; they laughed when you began buying 'worthless' prairie land; they laughed over in Oklahoma, I heard, when you put shoes on cows; and they laughed and said some things that weren't nice when you fenced your range. But since the blizzard they've even been scratching their heads a bit about *that*. Yes, and you were even smart enough to get the jump on Silent Shaw, something not many folks have ever been able to do, so far as I can ascertain."

"And in consequence, he's been causing me to do considerable jumping," Hardy remarked.

"So I gather," the sheriff commented dryly. "By the way, Sheriff East of Oldham County dropped in yesterday for a visit. He said there was one humdinger of a corpse and cartridge session in Tascosa a few weeks back. Six gents cashed in that they know of. Not sure about a bunch of four or five that went riding hell-for-election across the Canadian, apparently heading south. Looked like some of them had punctured hides. East said they *may* have come from New Mexico but he wasn't sure. Asked me if I'd heard anything about them from folks down here. I told him I hadn't. Wonder who those ridin' gents could have been?"

"I wonder," replied Hardy.

Sheriff Nance chuckled and did not pursue the subject.

"Where's Shaw going to set up in business, do you know?" Hardy suddenly asked.

"He bought the Ralston place on First Avenue and Washington Street," replied the sheriff. "Good big building; Ralston only used part of it. Shaw is knocking out partitions and putting in bigger windows. Reckon it'll be quite a show place when he's finished with it. Will open up under the new management in about ten days. Calls it The Coronado. And he bought a house over on Madison Street and has already moved his furniture down from Tascosa. Looks like he sure plans to make Amarillo his headquarters. Reckon he's holding on to his places in Dodge City, though."

"And his land down here too, eh?"

"Reckon he is," agreed Nance. "*If* he had your water, all that land would be mighty valuable; as it is, a lot of it isn't worth much."

"Yes, *if* he had it," Hardy repeated grimly.

"You can bet your last peso he isn't through trying to get it," the sheriff warned.

"He isn't sitting so pretty as he was in Oldham County, though," Hardy observed. "He didn't get you elected."

"Nope," the sheriff agreed. He added soberly, "But there's an election coming up, and you can bet that Shaw and his crowd and those who will gather around him will do their darnedest to get in their own man. Just watch!"

This possibility, not at all remote, gave Cliff Hardy food for considerable thought.

The practice of ranch owners hiring professional gunmen to guard their herds was again becoming alarmingly prevalent.

Everywhere on the Plains country were armed camps, and when various factions met in the towns they eyed each other with suspicion and distrust. Feeling was running so high that it was dangerous to be a neutral. All too often the honest small rancher was caught in the backwash of hatred and suspicion and knew not where to turn. He rode the range warily, and in town regarded all and sundry with watchful, smoldering eyes.

It was inevitable that Amarillo, situated as it was, should get its quota of questionable characters and factions hostile to one another. There were sporadic outbursts of violence, but nothing serious; Sheriff Nance was a cold proposition and a dead shot. He had served notice that he would tolerate no gunplay. Respect for the old peace officer's sterling character, acknowledged courage and skill with a gun kept things pretty well under control for the time being; but even Nance was not sanguine enough to believe that such desirable conditions would prevail indefinitely. Sooner or later Amarillo was due for trouble.

Besides, Sheriff Nance and his deputies could not spend all their time in Amarillo. They were kept pretty busy chasing rustlers, robbers and other miscreants, and in their absence, Amarillo was devoid of police protection. The town people had never gotten around to establishing a a city government, and law enforcement rested in the hands of the county authorities. The turbulent element knew this and acted accordingly.

The place Basset Shaw opened up on First Avenue was the finest of its kind in town. It boasted plate glass windows and a great mirror-blazing back bar pyramided with bottles of every shape and color. The bar stretched the full length of the room and was of real mahogany. The bartenders—usually four were on duty; at busy times five—wore white coats and ties and were adept at mixing drinks, although straight whiskey was still Amarillo's favorite tipple.

There were two roulette wheels, a faro bank, a chuck-a-luck game and poker tables. A long lunch counter opposite the bar served the best food obtainable, and circling the dance floor were tables for patrons who preferred to dine in greater comfort. The girls were good-looking and amiable and conducted themselves in a lady-like manner, at least on the dance floor, which was apparently as far as Shaw's interest in their conduct went.

On duty at all times were four floor men. They were watchful, hard-faced individuals whom Shaw had brought down from Dodge City. Nobody in Amarillo knew anything about their antecedents and they didn't do any talking about themselves.

"If they did, the chances are it would be awfully interesting hearing," commented Sheriff Nance. However, he could find no fault with the manner in which they conducted themselves, in the establishment or out of it.

"As usual, Shaw is looking to the future," the sheriff added. "His place is way beyond anything the town's present status justifies."

"But it'll be right in line before long," Cliff Hardy commented. "Folks are pouring in here all the time, and when the Sante Fe comes through from Carson City, as it will, and intersects the Denver and Fort Worth, giving Amarillo two railroads, you'll see a boom worth looking at."

"I've a notion you've got the right idea," agreed the sheriff. "Well, after that happens I expect we'll have some Rangers stationed here. And that'll make my job a bit easier, if Basset Shaw doesn't manage to ease me out of it next election."

CHAPTER XVII

It was Tommy Powers who inadvertently brought about the showdown between Cliff Hardy and Basset Shaw, with the able assistance of his bunky, Cale Klingman.

Powers was a carefree young puncher from the Nueces country. He was quick-tempered, a hard drinker and an inveterate gambler. Klingman was a year or two older but just as irresponsible. They were tophands, however, and Hardy thought well of them.

One day in early December, Powers and Klingman rode to Amarillo for a mite of diversion. They visited several saloons and finally drifted into Basset's place on First Avenue. They had several drinks and ended up occupying chairs at a poker table. The game was fairly steep; the players were three XIT and LS cowboys in for a bust, and one of Shaw's faro dealers, off duty, making up a full table.

Everything went along smoothly for a while, with the dealer the biggest winner and an LS hand not far behind. The saloon was fairly well crowded, although it was not quite dark, and bartenders and floor men were kept busy, the crowd being boisterous and a bit unruly.

Tommy Powers, though young in years, was old at poker, and he had keen eyes. He took to watching the dealer, who continued to win, in an unobtrusive way.

Without warning the ruckus cut loose. Powers suddenly leaned forward and grabbed the dealer's hand, whirling it palm up.

The dealer wore a plain gold ring on the third finger of his left hand, innocent-looking enough; but when Powers flipped his palm up, the ring showed a tiny mirror fitted to the underside of the band, by which the fellow could get a quick glimpse at the cards as he dealt them.

"Thought so!"_yelled Powers. "You blasted tinhorn!"

The dealer's right hand shot forward. A derringer slid from his sleeve and spatted against his palm.

But Powers was faster; his own gun was out, and with a slashing blow of the heavy barrel he knocked the dealer from his chair to lie unconscious, blood pouring from his split scalp.

Instantly the room was in an uproar. The floormen came bounding forward, but Klingman had his gun out now, and they recoiled before the two threatening muzzles.

Eyes shooting glances in every direction, the two cowboys scooped up their money, and what had been in front of the dealer, and pocketed it. Then they backed to the door, their guns menacing the crowd; nobody tried to stop them.

Powers and Klingman should have left Amarillo until things quieted down, but they didn't. They visited other saloons and proceeded to get roaring drunk, spreading the word of what had happened wherever they stopped, and finding plenty of interested listeners. Not that anybody outside of Shaw's Coronado was inclined to take what they said very seriously. Card game rows were of frequent occurrence, and it was always the other fellow who was in the wrong.

Two important facts the cowboys failed to take into consideration. One was that the badly hurt dealer had friends. The other that Basset Shaw always stood back of his men.

To make matters worse, Sheriff Nance was out of town at the moment. Otherwise, Powers and Klingman would have been sent back to the

Four Sixes to sober up.

Finally Powers and Klingman decided they'd go back to the Coronado for a last drink. They proceeded to do so, heading east, rather unsteadily, along Washington Street.

Just west of the saloon was a narrow alley. They were passing its mouth when guns blazed from the darkness. A slug burned its way along Klingman's ribs, knocking him sideways. Another turned his hat on his head. He jerked his Colt and fired blindly down the alley till the hammer clicked on an empty shell. Reloading as fast as he could, he suddenly realized that Powers was not beside him. The Nueces cowboy was lying on the ground, breathing in hoarse gasps, blood frothing his lips.

"Got me through the chest," he whispered as Klingman bent over him, and lapsed into unconsciousness.

Klingman straightened up, suddenly cold sober. Faces were pressed against the Coronado windows, others peeped over the swinging doors; but nobody came out. For an instant Klingman debated shooting up the place, but decided that help for Powers should come first.

Klingman was a big man, Powers slight in build. Klingman picked up the wounded puncher and headed for the doctor's office, which was a short distance away. Five minutes later Powers was on a table and the doctor was working over him.

"I don't know," the doctor replied to Klingman's anxious query. "He's hard hit, but if I can get the bleeding stopped, maybe he'll pull through; it'll be touch and go. Klingman, you get out of here and tell Cliff Hardy what happened; he'll want to know."

It was not quite midnight when Klingman pulled his lathered horse to a halt in the ranchhouse yard. A light burned in the living room; Hardy was still up, conferring with Cameron. His face set in bleak lines as he listened to what Klingman had to say.

"Shaw's killers drygulched us, that's what they did," Klingman concluded. "Boss, shall we all ride over there and take that infernal rum hole apart?"

"You'll stay right here," Hardy told him. "And that goes for everybody else. I'll handle this thing myself, and I want to find all of you here when I come back. Shut up, Tom. I don't want you or anybody else with me."

Cliff Hardy was in a red rage as he rode away from the ranchhouse. This time Shaw had gone too far. There was going to be a showdown once for all, man to man. Had the shooting occurred in the saloon, as a result of the exposure of the crooked tinhorn, Hardy would have thought little of it. But the shooting from ambush was nothing less than premeditated murder.

It was long past midnight when Hardy reached town, but that didn't mean much; a good portion of Amarillo never slept. He tied his horse at a rack several doors down from the Coronado and on the opposite side of the street. He loosened his guns in their sheaths, flexed his fingers to take the stiffness from them and, after rubbing his hands together vigorously until they were warm, crossed the street and entered the saloon.

Due either to the lateness of the hour or the shooting, the crowd had pretty well thinned out. The four floor men stood in a little knot near the far end of the bar. They stared at Hardy as he walked in, hands close to his gun butts, but did not speak.

After a swift, all-embracing glance around the room, Hardy walked straight to the floor men.

"Where's Shaw?" he asked, his pale eyes fixed on their faces.

Still the men did not speak, and the silence in the room was deadly. One jerked his head toward a closed door that Hardy knew led to a back room.

Hardy walked to the door, his eyes never leaving their faces.

"Nobody goes in till I come out," he stated flatly. He opened the door and slipped through, closing it behind him. There was a key in the lock; he turned it, shooting the bolt.

Basset Shaw was seated at a table halfway across the room, which was well lighted by two bracket lamps. He rose to his feet as Hardy entered. The purplish gleam was in his strange eyes, but otherwise he was expressionless. Hardy walked forward till only the table separated them.

"Shaw," he said, "this time you went too far. You had one of my men murdered in cold blood. I'm here to call you on it. Fill your hand!"

Shaw continued to regard him, showing absolutely no emotion.

"I am unarmed," he said.

Hardy stared at him. "We'll take care of that," he replied. He drew his right-hand gun and cocked it. Shaw gazed at him impassively, apparently activated only by a mild curiosity.

"Step back two paces," Hardy told him. Under the threat of the black muzzle, Shaw obeyed.

"Now here's the way we'll do it," Hardy said. "I'm laying this iron on the table; then I'm stepping back two paces. When I give the word we'll grab for it. The one who gets it will be the lucky one." He placed the Colt on the table as he spoke.

Shaw continued to regard him. "Hardy," he said, "you're crazy."

"Maybe I am," Hardy conceded, "but that's the way it stands. If you're too yellow to play the game this way, I'll pistol-whip you within an inch of your life and then kick you out into the other room for everybody to see what kind of a skunk you are. It's up to you."

"Step back and give the word," Shaw said.

Hardy glided back, his eyes hard on Shaw's face. "Go!" he barked.

Together they dived for the gun. Shaw, despite his bulk, was quick as a cat. His hand reached the table a fraction before Hardy's. He got the Colt by the butt; Hardy got it by the barrel. In grim silence they wrenched and struggled, Shaw endeavoring to bring the muzzle in line with the rancher, Hardy trying to wrench the weapon from Shaw's grasp. The sharp sight sliced Hardy's hand to the bone, blood streamed to make the barrel wet and slippery but he held on. He twisted hard, the gun exploded, the bullet ripping through the brim of his hat. Over went the table with a crash. A chair splintered to matchwood under their feet. To and fro they reeled and staggered. Shaw's greater bulk forced

Hardy back against the door. With his left hand he launched a vicious blow at the other's face. Hardy jerked his head aside, and Shaw's fist merely grazed his jaw. He could have gone for his left-hand gun, but that wasn't part of the bargain. It was the bloody Forty-five they fought for, or nothing. Shaw's strength was the strength of a maniac, and his greater weight began to tell. Their breath came in hoarse pants, their features were convulsed with strain. The purplish gleam was in Shaw's eyes as the gun muzzle slowly came around. Another instant and it would be in line with the rancher's face. Hardy heard the ominous double click as Shaw managed to cock the weapon again.

Hardy flung up his left hand, the fingers extended rigid. He chopped down with all his strength, the edge of his hand catching Shaw on the wrist with terrible force. Shaw's fingers flew open and Hardy wrenched the gun from his grasp. He flipped it, the butt slapping into his palm. Shaw had staggered back a few paces. Now he stood perfectly still as the gun muzzle lined on his heart. Hardy's eyes flashed with triumph. If ever a man deserved to die, Basset Shaw did. Cliff's fingers curled around the trigger.

But the finger had developed a strange wooden

feeling, had a tendency to straighten out. He tried to wet his dry lips with a tongue that seemed suddenly too big for his mouth. There was a terrible tightening of his stomach muscles, a feeling of suffocation in his chest. Cold sweat popped out on his cheeks and streamed down his face. Shaw stood motionless, waiting.

Again Hardy tried to bring pressure to bear on the trigger of the cocked gun, but his finger stubbornly refused to obey the impulses of his brain. He glared at Shaw over the gun barrel that wavered a little.

Basset Shaw broke the awful silence. "Hardy," he said, his voice flat and toneless, "I don't believe you're a killer, after all."

Hardy stared at him, his face working.

"Shaw, you're right!" he said thickly at last. He uncocked his gun and holstered it. Turning, he flipped the key in the lock, opened the door and stepped warily into the hushed saloon, where men stood rigid.

Sheriff Frank Nance was just coming through the swinging doors, a double-barrel sawed-off shotgun cradled in the crook of his arm. He regarded Hardy curiously.

"Well," he said, "did you kill him?"

"No," Hardy answered. He walked past the sheriff and out of the saloon. A moment later hoofs clattered, fading swiftly into the distance.

After pausing at the doctor's office to learn that Powers was still alive and the doctor a bit more hopeful, Cliff Hardy rode home in a black and bitter mood. A great cloud of depression had settled down on him, and he felt frustrated, futile, and utterly baffled by his own reactions. Why hadn't he killed Shaw? Shaw had a killing coming, there was no doubt in Hardy's mind as to that. And he, Hardy, had played the game in line with their agreement, only he had failed to claim forfeit. Shaw had been ready to pay; all he would have had to do was pull the trigger and the score would have been even and Shaw out of the way for good.

"But I couldn't! Hang it all, I couldn't!" he shouted aloud to the unresponsive night.

And now Shaw would continue his sinister machinations with greater freedom than before, being convinced that Hardy wouldn't kill him no matter what he did.

CHAPTER XVIII

Hardy slept for several hours; then, after grabbing a bite to eat, he rode to town to see about Powers. He found the young puncher weak, but conscious and in good spirits.

"Take better shooting than that to kill me," he whispered. "I'll be up and looking for that gunslinging gent before you know it, if I can just find out who he is. Maybe I ought to have hit that tinhorn a bit harder."

"I gather you hit him hard enough as it was," Hardy replied. "You just take it easy and stop bothering your head about him. When can we take the young hellion back to the ranch, Doc?"

"Give him a week and you can move him," the doctor replied. "He's going to pull through, all right, which I didn't expect when he was brought in. He'll be around looking for a chance to get hanged in a month, maybe less."

After leaving the hospital, Hardy dropped in to see Sheriff Nance. The old peace officer gave him a peculiar look.

"Well," he said, "you seem plumb anxious to get yourself killed. Of all the fool stunts I ever heard of, that was the limit. Why the blazes did you do it?"

"Didn't seem to be anything else to do, under the circumstances," Hardy defended his action.

"Maybe not, but it still doesn't make sense to me," said the sheriff.

"How'd you hear about it?" Hardy wondered. "Was somebody peeking through a crack?"

"No, I reckon everybody had too much sense to get close to that door," said Nance. "Basset Shaw told me about it."

"Basset Shaw!"

"That's right," said the sheriff. "He's a queer duck, and you never can tell what he'll take it into his head to do. For once in his life he seemed plumb eager to talk. He paid me a visit this morning. I thought he'd come in to prefer a charge against you, but he didn't. He just told me what happened. He wasn't accusing anybody, wasn't making any excuses, wasn't doing any explaining. Just seemed to want to set the record straight. Talked like a piece written for a newspaper. Stated the facts and let it go at that.

Yes, he's a queer duck and hard to figure. When he'd finished telling about it, he said he didn't tell anybody to shoot Powers. Said he didn't know a thing about it till after it had happened. Darned if I don't believe he was telling the truth."

"Wouldn't be surprised if he was," Hardy admitted wearily. "I don't think he'd take the trouble to lie about anything."

"The fact that that tinhorn Powers had the trouble with trailed his twine sometime last night sort of backs up what Shaw said," the sheriff added. "When he got his senses back he went out cussing. Said he was going to the doctor to get his head plastered, but he never showed up at McChesney's office. Reckon he got on Powers' trail and laid for him."

"Quite likely," Hardy agreed. "Well, it looks like I'm right back where I started. Shaw is on the loose and still all set to make trouble."

"Maybe he'll sort of hold up a bit from now on," Nance said hopefully. "Wouldn't be surprised if you gave him considerable of a jolt last night. He sort of intimated that when you lined that gun on him he looked across into eternity, and figured it wasn't far."

"When I lined it, I figured it would be an awful short hop," Hardy said grimly, "only somehow it didn't work out that way."

"I've a notion it was for the best," said the sheriff. "With just the two of you in there and Shaw with no gun in his hand or on him, it wouldn't have looked so good. Everybody knows he never packs a gun while he's in his place. You would have had some explaining to do that wouldn't have sounded very convincing to a jury, and you've got something of a reputation which you haven't bettered during the past couple of years, even though you have appeared justified in everything you've done."

Hardy had to concede that the sheriff was right. And now that he had cooled down a bit, he was thankful that he didn't have to explain things to Rita; it would not have been a pleasant chore.

"Shaw sure had a funny look on his face when I went into his back room last night," the sheriff continued reflectively. "I saw a look like that on a feller's face once before, over at the state prison. Feller was all set to be hanged, up on a scaffold, rope around his neck, and they were getting ready to slip the black cap over his face when a man came running in to tell the warden the governor had just granted a reprieve. I've a notion Shaw knew how that feller felt.

"I asked him what the shooting was about and

he said a gun went off accidental."

Although he was in no mood for mirth, Hardy had to grin.

"Guess the only time it went off was accidental, all right, luckily for me," he agreed. "What else did he say?"

"Nothing," the sheriff replied. "He just stood there looking down at a busted chair. I figured busting a chair wasn't exactly busting the law, so I came away. And, as I said, this morning he came to see me. So long! Try to keep out of trouble for a change."

A few days later the Four Sixes had an unexpected visitor. Cliff Hardy stood on the front porch watching the approach of a rider on a splendid bay horse. Suddenly he cleared the four steps at a bound and went racing down the driveway. The rider of the bay horse was Rita Sostenes.

"Well! this is a pleasant surprise!" he exclaimed as he lifted her lightly from the saddle, whooped for a wrangler to care for her horse and enveloped her small form in a bear hug. "What the devil brings you out here, darling? Shaw in trouble?"

"No, he's fine," she replied as soon as she got her breath. "I'm taking the train to Fort Worth day after tomorrow. My aunt, Dad's youngest sister—she isn't much older than me—is about due to have a baby. She's already got a couple of kids, and I'm going to ride herd on them till the new maverick is safely corralled. I just couldn't leave without telling you."

"I'm sure glad you didn't," he declared heartily, giving her another hug. "Come on in. Chuck's on the table. Hope you're hungry."

"Starved as usual," she replied. "I don't see why the devil I don't get fat as a butterball, the way I put it away, but I don't."

Supper at the Four Sixes was usually an hilarious affair. Tonight, however, the big dining room was about as gay as a funeral parlor. The conversation consisted chiefly of such remarks as, "Yes, I'll be much obliged for some butter," or, "Pass the bread, please," instead of the customary, "Slide along the grease!" or, "Throw me a hunk of sourdough, you lop-eared son of an unpedigreed canine!"

Rita stood it for about three minutes. Abruptly she laid down her knife and fork and hit the table a resounding blow with her small fist.

"Say!" she exploded to the slack-jawed punchers. "What is this, a dining table or a slab in the morgue? Listen, you, I was brought up with from fifteen to twenty herders around me.

They could swear in two languages, and our old Chinese cook could swear in three. I'm not going to bite anybody, and I'm not going to be shocked. I can out-cuss any of you if you get me started. I expect to have you around me the rest of my life, and I'm not going to put up with a bunch of tongue-tied ninnies. Loosen the latigos and be yourselves!"

Grins and chuckles went around the table. Soon the usual uproar was going full blast, and the Four Sixes hands were thoroughly enjoying their meal and the hour of relaxation it always provided.

After supper, Rita inspected the ranchhouse and voiced approval.

"You sure keep things in shape," she complimented old Pete.

"A man can do a better chore of housekeeping than any female," Pete declared, a benign expression on his wrinkled face.

"I think you're right. He can when he sets his mind to it," admitted Rita. "The trouble is most of them don't give a hoot. I want to see the bunkhouse."

"I ain't got nothing to do with that pigpen," Pete hurriedly protested. "I ain't responsible for what you'll find there."

Rita proceeded to the bunkhouse, after ordering Hardy to stay on the front porch where he was. A moment after she entered he heard a feminine voice exclaim:

"Heavenly days!"

Out the door cowhands shot like pips from a squeezed orange. Big Bill Jasper and Cale Klingman came hurrying to the porch.

"She wants a tub of hot water and a broom and a mop," the latter told Hardy. "Is it okay?"

"I've got nothing to do with this ruckus," Hardy hastily disclaimed. "Go see Pete, and fight it out with her."

That night, glancing around the spick-and-span bunkhouse, Bill Jasper remarked:

"I was scairt when the Boss got married everything would be spoiled for us, but now he can't do it too soon for my money."

There were sober nods of agreement, and Cale Klingman proceeded to pay Rita the highest compliment the rangeland had to offer.

"Yes," said Klingman, "she's a gal to ride the river with!"

Rita made no mention of the happenings in Amarillo the week before. Hardy deduced she had not heard about them, and did not broach the subject.

"Your uncle know you rode out here?" he asked when they were alone in the ranchhouse.

"Sure," she replied. "I told him."

"What did he say?"

"Nothing. He just nodded. He never tells me what I can do or can't do; he's nice that way."

"Seems to me he'd have been sort of surprised," Hardy commented.

"I don't think so," Rita replied. "I told him you came to see me in Tascosa. He didn't seem surprised at that, either. In fact, I don't think anything ever surprises him. And," she added, "I really don't think he has a thing against you personally. It's just that you've got something he wants, and he feels it's right for him to take anything he wants if he can get it."

"Well, *he's* got something *I* want," Hardy retorted.

"Oh, no he hasn't," Rita replied cheerfully. "You know better than that. You've got me, darn it, roped and hogtied, and you know it."

Hardy rode to Amarillo with Rita the following morning. After he kissed her goodbye at Shaw's house on Madison Street, he repaired to Doc McChesney's office to see how Tommy Powers was making out.

"You can take him out to the spread any time you want to," Doc said. "He's coming along fine, thanks chiefly to first class nursing. That niece of Basset Shaw's, Rita Sostenes, has been here looking after him the past four days. She's a natural born nurse."

Hardy stared at the doctor. "Well, I'll be hanged!" he muttered. "And she didn't say a word about it!"

"She's a wonder!" Powers broke in enthusiastically. "Boss, you sure know how to pick 'em!"

"Uh-huh, but why the devil did she have to pick Basset Shaw for an uncle?" Hardy complained.

"She didn't pick him," old Doc observed sagely. "Folks don't pick their relations, or quite a few people wouldn't have any kin folks at all. We can pick our friends; relations are wished on us, sometimes as a punishment for our sins, I think."

Hardy left the doctor's office rather dazedly. Tom Cameron is right, he told himself. Any man who thinks he knows a single thing about women needs to have his head examined.

CHAPTER XIX

Cliff Hardy's bone wagons still ranged far and wide across the bare brown prairie. The great harvest of bones was nearly over, the deposits now few and far between. Besides, much land was now privately owned. Often it would take a wagon several days to get a load. However, picking still paid and the money was welcome in the season when no shipping herds took the trail. Hardy decided to keep his wagons rolling for as long as they could show a profit. He figured that by early spring at the latest it would not pay to search the prairie further; but in the spring his first shipping herd would be ready to take the trail, and another and larger one would be ready for the fall or beef roundup.

"We'll have plenty of critters by the time it begins to get warm," Tom Cameron predicted; "and the price of cows will be up, what with the blizzard losses and everything. We're one of the few lucky ones. That blizzard and the one following, though it wasn't as bad as the first, raised ructions with plenty of spreads. Well, it's a worthless blizzard that blows nobody good."

"It's a pity folks had to have trouble, but it will shoot the price of beef up," Hardy admitted. "Just the same, I hope nothing else bad happens. One more whack and a lot of little fellows will go under."

"I expect the worst is over for this year," Cameron replied cheerfully. "Maybe another storm or two, but that should be about all."

It was Cale Klingman who brought some interesting news to the Four Sixes.

"Basset Shaw is running cows onto his west pasture," Cale announced on his return from a trip to town.

"Well, there's no reason why he shouldn't," Hardy observed. "He's got enough water over there to take care of a good-sized herd. Glad to hear he's turning his hand to something constructive."

"Maybe he's decided to settle down and stop raising ned," hazarded Cameron.

"Maybe," Hardy said without conviction.

A week later Cameron brought a news item of more serious import relative to the activities of Basset Shaw.

"Cliff," he said, "those cows Shaw brought in are longhorns from the Devil's River country."

Hardy looked grave. "You sure?" he asked.

"Yes, I'm sure," Cameron replied. "I worked down there once and I know the brands. Shaw has run his Rafter S on them, but I got a look at a couple of the blotted brands where the iron hadn't been handled neatly and I could make out the original Flying O plain as anything. Shaw must have bought them from the Flying O spread. It's a big one and they usually have plenty of stock to dispose of. You'd think he'd know better than to bring those Devil's River cows up here."

"Maybe he does and just doesn't give a hoot," Hardy commented grimly. "Either way, he's liable to make trouble for other spreads. I heard the XIT are bringing in South Texas cattle, but their range is fenced."

"Just the same, they're taking a chance," said Cameron. "Everybody knows, or should know, that South Texas cows, especially those from the Devil's River country, carry Spanish fever ticks. Those old mossy backs from down there are just about immune to Spanish fever, but they pack the ticks with them."

Cliff Hardy spent sleepless nights trying to decide what to do about it. He knew perfectly

well that he was facing potential ruin. Let the
fever strike his herd and he would very likely
lose every head. Certainly the Herefords, and it
was highly improbable that even the longhorns
were immune to the ravages of the disease; even
hardy South Texas longhorns become immune
to tick fever only through long association with
the disease.

From time to time there could be seen, far
across the prairie, the moving dots that were the
Devil's River longhorns. Normally the cows
would not roam so far from their scanty water
supply to the west, but in the cold weather they
tended to graze over a much wider area. And
there was no telling what some mavericking
critter might take it into its head to do. Any
morning Hardy might awake to find a dozen
rubbing against his posts; he went cold all over
at the thought. He gave strict orders that any
cow approaching the wire should be instantly
shot.

But that was a dubious preventive measure.
The ticks would quite likely leave the cattle before the animal could be burned and, unde-
tected, make their way through the grass to his
range.

It was the thought of burning the carcasses,
the only safe way to dispose of them, that gave

Hardy his idea. He called his range boss to a conference.

"Tom," he said, "I've got a plan that I believe will work; something I've been thinking about for some time as a guard against grass fires. You know some bad ones sweep up this way from the southwest every now and then. I saw one back in the early '80's; it killed a lot of cows and destroyed a lot of buildings."

"What's the plan?" asked Cameron.

"Just this," Hardy replied. "You know Spanish ticks won't leave the grass. The grass can be full of them all around a bare spot of ground, and there won't be a single tick on the bare spot. Here's my idea: we'll hire Bill Metcalf, who built most of the XIT fence, and his big gang plows. We'll have him plow three furrows all along our west wire and along the south wire to the creek. That will keep out the ticks, and it isn't likely that a grass fire will jump the furrows. So we'll be safeguarding ourselves against two dangers."

"Feller, you *are* smart!" applauded Cameron. "That'll take care of it. I'll ride to Amarillo tomorrow and see Metcalf. He'll be glad to take over the chore; this isn't his busy time of year."

It took Metcalf and his enormous plows less than a week to do the job. The plows were drawn by six mules. One plow was followed by another a few yards behind and a little to the side, the second followed by a third. When the earthen guard was finally set up, Hardy had little fear of either fire or the deadly ticks.

Shortly before Christmas, Hardy received a letter from Rita. Among other things, mostly personal, she wrote:

"My aunt had her baby all right, but she isn't in very good shape, so I guess I'll have to stick around for a spell. Hope it won't be long."

Hardy hoped so, too, but under the circumstances there wasn't anything much he could do about it. He contemplated a trip to Fort Worth if she was unduly delayed.

It was natural that the Four Sixes bunch watched Shaw's activities with interest.

"He's sure going into business, all right," reported Bill Jasper. "He's dredging out waterholes fed by the little crick from the big springs on his north pasture, and he's building a ranchhouse and a bunkhouse about five miles out from town. I heard he brought quite a few of the hands down from his Kansas spread. Don't know where he got the rest of them; I got a look at some of them, and they're a salty bunch. They were in Amarillo this afternoon, six or seven of 'em, and they were sticking together and didn't have much to say to anybody."

"Not unusual for strangers in a community," Hardy observed.

"Uh-huh, that's right," agreed Jasper, "but they sort of gave me the impression that they didn't figure to have anything much to do with anybody. Different from strangers who, while they don't know anybody much, are willing to get acquainted. I don't think that bunch wants to know anybody, and they sure had an eye out for everything going on around 'em. Sort of reminded me of the time I saw Billy the Kid and Doc Skurlock and their bunch of hellions in Tascosa. They acted just that way, which wasn't unnatural with somebody gunning for them all the time. Oh, they're cowhands, all right, but I figure they don't pack their irons— several of them were packing a pair—just to shoot rattlesnakes with."

"Shaw's liable to need them," grunted Cale Klingman. "I tell you there's some mighty mean talk going around. The little fellows were riled up enough when the XIT brought those South Texas cows in. Some of them say the XIT did it deliberately in their fight against the small ranchers, but those cows are behind wire, while Shaw's are mavericking around on open range."

"Would be just like Shaw to do that sort of

thing to cause trouble," declared Jasper. "I wouldn't put it past him."

Cliff Hardy listened without comment to the gabble of his hands, but his black brows drew together.

A couple of quiet weeks followed, and then disaster struck. Southwest of Shaw's holdings was a small ranch, the Triangle Dot, owned by a former Brazos River cattleman named Burton Powell. Spanish fever broke out in the Triangle Dot herd.

There was no doubt as to the nature of the disease that afflicted Powell's cows; all the characteristic symptoms were present—red urine, yellow mucous membranes, and rapid loss of strength.

A wave of terror swept the section. The ranches, many of which had already suffered heavy losses from the blizzard, saw themselves facing ruin. Powell insisted that the authorities do something about it, that Shaw be forced to remove his cattle or destroy them.

But it was pointed out that there was no proof that Shaw was responsible for the plague, that the XIT and the LS had brought in South Texas cattle some time previous, and that Powell's west pasture ran to the XIT fence. Until it was definitely established that the Rafter S cows were the offenders, nothing could be done.

Powell, young and hot-headed, decided to take the law in his own hands, and he found plenty willing to join him in the affray. At night, most of the Rafter S cattle bunched near the waterholes and the stream that ran from the springs. So under cover of darkness the raiders, nearly fifty strong, rode to the Rafter S and began shooting the cows. They had hardly opened fire, however, when there came a hail of bullets from the thickets and rocks adjoining the springs. The Rafter S had been warned of the raiders coming, and Shaw's salty punchers were determined to protect their stock.

The raiders fought back, but the Rafter S bunch had the advantage of position and they were forced to withdraw sullenly, leaving behind three of their number, two of them Powell's hands, who would never raid again. The bodies, and an account of the affair, were delivered to the sheriff's office the next morning.

Powell and several companions rode to Amarillo and demanded that the killers be brought to justice; but Sheriff Nance told them bluntly:

"You fellers haven't a leg to stand on. You were trespassing on Shaw's land and destroying his cattle. He had every right to protect his property. My advice to you is to tighten the latigoes on your jaws. If Shaw is of a mind to, he can prosecute every one of you known to have had a hand in the business."

Next a delegation of owners called on Shaw with angry protests and threats. Shaw patiently heard them out.

"Gentlemen," he said then, "before my herd took the trail north, every head was dipped in a vat containing a solution strong enough to kill the ticks; as you all know, this is an accredited practice. My herd was then cleared by the inspectors. I will concede the remote possibility of an infected animal joining the herd, or that a cow might have been missed being dipped. But there is something you appear to be overlooking —the time element. You all know when my herd arrived in this section, and those of you who have had experience with tick fever must know that too short a period has elapsed for the disease, if contracted from my stock, to make its appearance. But," he added significantly, "the cattle brought in by the XIT have been here plenty long enough."

There were men in the delegation who had had experience with the fever, and they were forced to admit the validity of Shaw's contention.

"Yes, he talked himself out of it," Tom Cameron reported to Hardy. "Was he really right about the time it takes for the fever to show up?"

"Tom, I don't know," Hardy admitted frankly. "But it seems to me those fellows who have had experience with the fever should know, and it appears they agreed with Shaw. Well, thank the Lord we're on the sidelines in this particular row, so far."

A little later, however, he remarked thoughtfully, "But what I imagine those fellows are overlooking now is that Shaw hasn't been given a clean bill of health. Dipping is all right to kill the ticks, if the solution is strong enough; but if it's too strong, it raises ned with the cows. So there's always a good chance that it will be too weak. The XIT cows were supposed to have been dipped, too, but just the same we've got Spanish fever in the section. So it's up to us to take no chances."

"You're right," agreed Cameron, and rode off to make sure the patrols were on the job.

CHAPTER XX

It was Tom Cameron who first saw the great brown-tinged cloud climbing up the south-western horizon, the early morning sun rays glinting amber and gold on its edges. He called Hardy, who was busy with some accounts in the living room. Together they watched the ominous billows climb higher and higher.

"It's a grass fire and a big one, that's what it is," Hardy quickly decided. "It's coming up from the south and a bit to the west. Let's get up on the roof, and maybe we can spot it better."

From the greater elevation they were able to see a long way across the prairie.

"Yes, it's a fire all right," Hardy repeated. "Coming fast, too; must be considerable wind back of it. Tom, this is going to be bad."

"Think our range is safe?" Cameron asked nervously.

"Yes, I think it is," Hardy replied. "Very unlikely the flames will jump the plow. We may lose a few fence posts, but I expect that will be all. Most of the grass right outside the fence is buffalo grass and low. I figure the real bad blaze won't come within a hundred yards of our line at any point. But farther to the west, where the growth is mostly needle and wheat, belly-high on a horse, gentlemen, hush!"

"It'll sweep Shaw's holdings," Cameron predicted.

"Yes, he'll very likely lose his new ranchhouse," Hardy agreed. "But if his hands are on the job, they'll shove the stock north into the canyons this side of the river and have a good chance to save most of the cows. Plenty of barren gulches and dry washes up there. Look! They're already at work."

Far to the west could be seen dancing blobs that were undoubtedly hard-riding horsemen. Other squatter blobs were cattle the punchers were rounding up and shoving north. Hardy watched the activity for some minutes, his brows drawing together. He raised his eyes to the dark cloud in the sky. It was much nearer and was changing from a uniform expanse of rusty brown. Columns and pillars surged upward. Wavering outposts of fire-flecked black sped on either side.

Under the darkening cloud a vast stillness reigned. It was as though the earth lay dead beneath its pall. And the bright sunlight was dimming.

Hardy's glance dropped to the hurrying dots far to the west. His lips tightened.

"Tom," he said, "we've got to give those fellows a hand. We'll leave five men here, including Pete, to keep a watch on things. The fire is running almost due north, and they shouldn't have any trouble keeping pace with it and smashing out any brands that might happen to blow over the plow. The rest of us will ride over there and do what we can to help Shaw's hands."

"That son doesn't deserve any help from anybody, let alone from you," growled Cameron. "I say to let him roast."

"Might be a good idea," Hardy conceded, "but his boys are cowmen and, for all we know to the contrary, may be all right. Besides, the Rafter S cows haven't done anything to deserve to get barbecued before their time. Let's go!"

Ten minutes later Hardy and his men were galloping across the prairie, where wisps of smoke were already swirling and curdling. As they drew near the beleaguered Rafter S punchers, greetings were waved; there was no need to comment or ask questions. It was the code of the rangeland: although you might be at outs with your neighbor, when the common enemy, nature, struck, you rallied to his assistance. Soon the Four Sixes cowboys were busy combing out cattle and shoving them north.

As he worked farther west, Hardy caught sight of a bulky figure mounted on a big roan; it was Basset Shaw.

"Came to lend you a hand," Hardy shouted.

"Nice of you," replied Shaw, and turned back to the business of swerving a bunch of recalcitrant longhorns in the right direction.

By common but unspoken agreement, the two owners worked together, combing the thickets and driving forth the cows that had sought dubious shelter there, slanting them across the prairie to where the main body of the hands was bunching the herd and pushing it toward the safety of the canyons and draws. Now the air was thick with smoke, and embers were beginning to fall.

Farther and farther to the west they worked in the deepening murkiness. Glancing back, Hardy uttered an exclamation.

"Shaw," he called, "we've got to get out of this. The fire's jumped. On the east and west it's ahead of us, and coming up fast behind."

He was right. The wind, which was blowing from the southwest, had freshened. The fire was coming on at race-horse speed. They were in the center of a flaming crescent, the horns of which were probing northward well in front of them. Abruptly they were in serious danger.

"Come on," said Shaw; "we'll have to ride for it. Maybe we can make it to the canyon in time."

The frightened horses needed no urging and sped north at a rapid gait. Hardy was forking a good bay; he had not cared to risk Rojo's legs in the gruelling task of combing out the unpredictable longhorns and had left him on the Four Sixes stable. But the bay was a reliable cayuse and the equal of Shaw's mount.

On they rode at top speed, but urge their horses as they would, the grass fire travelled a little faster. Brands were showering all around, and wherever one landed in a patch of dry grass, a flicker instantly sprang up. The smoke was so thick that breathing was difficult, and the swirling ash made them sneeze and cough constantly.

They had covered perhaps three miles when the broken country loomed ahead, dimly seen through the smoke clouds. Hardy began to believe they might make it, after all. But when they reached the chaparral that grew out for several hundred yards from the broken cliffs, it proved to be a close and thorny tangle through which no horse could hope to force its way. And the growth was dry as tinder; it would provide no obstacle for the fire. Rather, it would but increase its intensity. And there was no time to ride along the frowning bristle in search of a possible opening.

"We'll have to try it on foot," Hardy shouted. "Without our weight, maybe the horses can make it in the clear."

Shaw nodded and swung from the saddle; Hardy did likewise. Freed of their burden, the horses dashed madly eastward, parallelling the wall of growth, their speed greatly increased, and were quickly lost in the smoke.

"Yes, maybe they'll make it," Hardy muttered. "Which is more than we're likely to do," he added grimly.

With the strength of despair they tackled the growth, forcing their way through, heedless of thorns, often crawling on their hands and knees between the close-spaced trunks, choking with the smoke, gasping and panting. Before they had gone a hundred yards they heard an ominous snapping and crackling behind them; the flames had reached the chaparral and it was burning fiercely.

On and on they went, their strength ebbing, their movements becoming erratic, uncertain.

Hardy felt a numb despair, a feeling of utter impotence gripping him. He began to care little what happened. Anything would be better than this fiery torture, this exhausting effort.

And then without warning they were at the base of the cliffs up to which the growth extended unbroken. The wall of dark stone rose sheer for more than a score of feet. Frantically they sidled along it, seeking a spot where it could be climbed, and finding none. The fire was less than a hundred yards behind them now and surging forward.

Finally Hardy paused where a slight fissure scored the surface of the sheer stone. It was but a narrow crack, less than three feet wide at the base and some seven feet in height, and narrowing to a few inches. He eyed it doubtfully.

"Just the same I've a notion a man snugged in there might live through it," he said. "But there's only room for one. In you go, Shaw."

"Reckon not," Shaw returned imperturbably. "Nobody gives a hoot if I live or die, but there's somebody waiting for you. You're going in."

"Like fury I am!" Hardy exploded. "Listen—"

"Look there!" Shaw suddenly exclaimed, pointing to the left.

Hardy turned his head, and Shaw hit him

with all the weight of his big body behind the blow. His fist crashed against Hardy's jaw, and Cliff went down like a pole-axed steer. Shaw unemotionally picked up his limp body, carried him to the cliff and jammed him into the crevice as far as was possible. He made sure he was wedged so tight he wouldn't tumble out. Then he turned to face the leaping flames, now less than a dozen yards distant. The choking smoke swirled about him; his sweat-drenched shirt was steaming and charred from the blistering heat. He drew a cigar from his pocket and lighted it. He dragged hard and blew out the smoke, rolling the cigar from one corner of his mouth to the other. Then with a steady step he walked forward to meet the rushing wall of flame.

It was the pain flowing through his scorched hands and face that brought Cliff Hardy back to consciousness. For a few dazed moments he couldn't understand where he was or what had happened to him, or what it was that cramped his aching shoulders like a vice. Most of his shirt was burned off and his chest was blistered. Finally realization bored through the fog that clouded his brain. He wrenched free from the constricting stone and stumbled out of the crevice.

Before him was a smoking waste where embers still flickered. The cliff face was seamed and blistered from the heat and still hot. And a few yards from its base lay a burned and blackened thing that once had been a man.

On wavering feet he stumbled to Shaw's body and gazed down at it. His clearing mind reconstructed what had happened.

"Knocked me out and shoved me into the crack," he mumbled, feeling of his swollen jaw. He stooped down and, summoning all his strength, lifted the pitiful remains. With drunken steps he reeled and staggered back to the cliff and shoved Shaw's body into it, wedging it tight and managing to fold the skeletal hands over the shrivelled breast. Then, working slowly and methodically, with the jerky movements of an automaton, he collected boulders almost too hot to touch from the cliff base. Painfully and precisely he walled up the crevice until there was no opening large enough to admit a prowling animal. He stepped back, trembling from head to foot, and gazed at Basset Shaw's tomb.

"A hard man," he muttered aloud, "hard and bad; but a man to ride the river with!"

A wave of nausea swept over him, and he sank

slowly to the ground to lie in a stupor of utter exhaustion. Hours passed before he was able to struggle to his feet again, clutching the cliff face for support. Then, with a last glance at the "grave" of the man who had given his life that Cliff might live, he turned and stumbled south through the choking ash. He was far out on the blackened prairie and the sullen red sun was near the smoky horizon when he saw horsemen riding toward him.

They were several of the Rafter S and Four Sixes hands, including Tom Cameron. In terse, flat sentences he told them what had happened. They got him on a horse and took him to town and the doctor. Later, swathed in oiled bandages, he retold the story to Sheriff Frank Nance.

The old peace officer heard him out in silence; then he said, in his peculiarly deep and resonant voice:

"Our Lord died that others might have eternal life, and I've a notion that, no matter how much there is against Shaw, He won't be too hard on a man who gave his life that another might live. God rest his soul!"

The following afternoon, Cliff Hardy met the train that brought Rita home in answer to his telegram. She cried a little when he recounted Basset Shaw's tragic and heroic death, but managed to smile at him through her tears.

"I think it was for the best," she said. "He was not happy."

"Yes, I've a notion maybe it was," Hardy agreed. "Folks will forget the other things, but they'll never forget the way he died."

Two days later, Cliff Hardy stood on the ranchhouse porch, his young wife beside him, and gazed over the broad rangeland that was the symbol of his achievement. He had fought and won against the opposition of men, disease, and the dumb, imponderable forces of nature. In his heart was a quiet contentment.

"Reckon we'll have to move the fences a bit, honey," he said. "The land over there is yours now."

"Cliff," she replied, "if it's all right with you, we'll leave the fences right where they are. We have all we need here. The rest we'll sell, at a reasonable price, to people who will be glad to have it."

"That's a nice notion, all right," Hardy instantly agreed. "They can run ditches from the creek and get plenty of water. It'll be fine for folks who want to build homes and raise some kids."

"Just like we'll do." She smiled at him. "We'll want a flock of little bone pickers, and they'll need some other kids to play with."

GET 4 FREE BOOKS!

You can have the best Westerns delivered to your door for less than what you'd pay in a bookstore or online. Sign up for one of our book clubs today, and we'll send you 4 FREE* BOOKS, worth $23.96, just for trying it out...**with no obligation to buy, ever!**

Authors include classic writers such as **LOUIS L'AMOUR, MAX BRAND, ZANE GREY** and more; plus new authors such as **COTTON SMITH, JOHNNY D. BOGGS, DAVID THOMPSON** and others.

As a book club member you also receive the following special benefits:
- **30% off all orders!**
- **Exclusive access to special discounts!**
- **Convenient home delivery and 10 days to return any books you don't want to keep.**

Visit **www.dorchesterpub.com**
or call
1-800-481-9191

There is no minimum number of books to buy, and you may cancel membership at any time.
*Please include $2.00 for shipping and handling.